ALSO BY JAMES McCOURT

Mawrdew Czgowchwz

KAYE
WAYFARING
IN "AVENGED"

KAYE
WAYFARING
in
"AVENGED"

Four stories by

JAMES McCOURT

ALFRED A. KNOPF   NEW YORK   1984

Copyright © 1983, 1984 by James McCourt

All rights reserved under International and Pan-American
Copyright Conventions. Published in the United States by
Alfred A. Knopf, Inc., New York, and simultaneously in Canada
by Random House of Canada Limited, Toronto. Distributed by
Random House, Inc., New York.

Portions of this work were previously published in *Grand Street*.

Grateful acknowledgment is made to the following for
permission to reprint previously published material:

CBS Songs: Lyrics from "Once in a Lifetime" by Gus Kahn and
Walter Donaldson from the film *Operator 13*, 1934. Copyright
1934, renewed 1961 by Metro-Goldwyn-Mayer Corporation.
Rights assigned to CBS Catalogue Partnership. All rights
controlled and administered by CBS Robbins Catalog, Inc. All
rights reserved. International copyright secured. Used by
permission.

Famous Music Corporation: Lyrics from "Low Down Lullaby"
by Leo Robin and Ralph Rainger from the film *Little Miss
Marker*, 1934. Copyright 1934 by Famous Music Corporation.
Copyright renewed 1961 by Famous Music Corporation.

Library of Congress Cataloging in Publication Data

McCourt, James
Kaye Wayfaring in "Avenged."

I. Title.
PS3563.C3448K3   1984   813'.54   83-49088
ISBN 0-394-52361-x

Manufactured in the United States of America

FIRST EDITION

For V.

KAYE
WAYFARING
IN "AVENGED"

SITTING shivering in time, Kaye Wayfaring brooded. The peak fall day enhanced her. She considered impetus. October gleamed as it chilled the town. She considered the approach of winter, of the holiday season. Yuletide: completion. She considered the picture.

Time pressed. *Avenged*, a costly venture, lingered in production. There they all were, over that way in a sunken russet glade, occupied in setting up another shot—for Panavision, for art, for success (a decent enough program). A stretch of morainal plateau in the Ramble had been redressed, enhanced. From a promontory just across the gulf from the rock on which Kaye sat slouched, a cascade had been installed, feeding into the Gill, causing it to appear torrential. Gaffers exerted themselves, hauling cable and taping down marks. The key grip smoked a Real. The Best Boy knowingly exchanged trade news with idle go-fers.

Kaye decided *Avenged* might just turn out if—as always, if—she plunged, obeying a charged impulse. Smiling, smoking raw Luckies, on her rock high in the Ramble, overlooking the still, leaf-cloaked pond, she thought: Plunge like the Lorelei, like the Rhine maidens (Wellgunde, Woglinde, Flosshilde, and Kaye), like Ondine, like Russalka. If only she plunged, darting down into *Avenged*. Yet, as had been said of one of Houdini's efforts, "Failure means a drowning death." Kaye Wayfaring, one valiant trouper, weighed Candace, her role, the creature: What is there of me in you, you extravagant, driven witch?

One sure way to play Candace, Kaye knew, was the same way she had phoned in the last few performances. "Wayfaring's icy panache!" Any unit publicist could (must, lately, it appeared) trumpet that quality—the haughty, bewildered, vaguely bruised quality. Kaye had no more use for it. Where in the Wayfaring economy was *it?*

Kaye Wayfaring regrouped her forces, seeking: What must I do? What must I? Am I played out? Two words, conjoined, cheered her: "much vaunted."

Her mother, Cordelia Bridgewood Wayfaring, an amateur of consequence, had said, "If you're going to be a talking woman, be a triumphant talking woman. Be purposeful, generous; be all you dare. Might as well go at it tooth and nail."

"So saying, she plunged to her death," Kaye mumbled, repeating an old Yale Drama School refrain, then quickly recoiled from the expression and from the recall it and the torrent produced.

Well, what was the key to *it?*

Above all, she longed to become precise: to give specific information.

Things written about her terrified her.

"Wayfaring understands that no star actress wears anybody else's old hair," her director, Orphrey Whither, had assured the attendant press.

"Wayfaring is honest in the most arduous way, and in the old, perfect manner. She understands, as Mrs. Siddons and Peg Woffington apparently did, that honesty is the mark of the star," an enthusiast had scribbled in *Film-opinion.*

"Wayfaring understands that stardom is necessarily vexing. Stars never rest: they merely, occasionally, lounge,"

Goneril Dreene had grandly announced in *Pomander Walk.*

"Wayfaring keeps her interior voyages to herself. Stardom demands secrecy," some wag had snapped, pretending an intimacy.

H.Q.P., that seasoned, trusted metropolitan arbiter and public scold, had ventured to write of Kaye Wayfaring: "So *on*, so *forth:* vivid and particular. No actress in these past two weary decades has displayed so deft a form. Wayfaring does *deliver*—in the Sullavan-Stanwyck-Lombard-Davis tradition, with offhand, odd resemblances to, among others, Irene Dunne, Frances Farmer, and, eerily, Jeanne Eagels. Kaye Wayfaring is something of a navigator. *Impetus* is her concern."

Kaye Wayfaring sat perplexed. Others' names surrounded hers: they threatened suffocation. All Kaye could say was "I'll have you know . . ."

Shading her fortunate eyes, she considered what she had termed, self-mockingly, "the plan"—a degree-by-degree personal overhaul, a concerted effort to improve the whole works. She had her qualms: Am I to turn out finally to have been entirely *fashioned?* Is one made up of spare parts? What about this *equipoise?* She brooded, she smoked, she considered *Avenged.*

The harried unit publicist's release for the first day of shooting had informed the industry: "Orphrey Whither's *Avenged,* based on a Diderot tale already once brought to the screen as *Les Dames du Bois de Boulogne* (Robert Bresson, director, France, 1944) and starring the blazing Kaye Wayfaring, two-time Oscar nominee (for *We Are Born, We Live, We Die* and for *Way Station*), is certain to provoke controversy. Such is the valence of the combined powers of Orphrey Whither, poet-scripter Jameson O'Maurigan, distinguished British National Theatre actor Patrick More, and Kaye Wayfaring that a new meaning is imparted on the screen to *revenge,* another dimension is revealed in the geometry of human lust. Never before has desire so bruised, so scalded so cruelly."

Good God, Kaye Wayfaring had wondered, what on earth is all that about? That passage offered no key to *it,* she could tell them. But then, to demand of publicity *keys* . . . Publicity was hearsay.

Kaye remembered an afternoon in the heated, sweated term of her adolescence, when, passing through languid days in the house on Warwoman Road in Clayton, Georgia, she had come upon herself full-face in the smudged upstairs-bathroom mirror while overhearing a conversation on the veranda below, and had told herself, They pass life discussing weather and traffic. They pass life by. They know no navigation. She had mourned them in advance of their letting life go and dying, while each night the incessant, troubled snoring sounded on as groups of besotted stayovers lay abed and Kaye lay wakeful on the tar roof of the veranda, clad in a lavender-blue silk kimono her father had salvaged from the ruins of imperial Japan, smoking Luckies, yearning to cross the road and spend the summer night stalking Warwoman Dell, questioning the starred firmament, not sure of much, but certain she would either die or up and out—and soon, at that, either way. She'd sit up smoking, scented with 4711, and braid her rust-red hair, thinking about decisions and feeling histrionic. Fuchsia hung in baskets, bougainvillea flourished in the scuppernong arbor (a scion of her aunt Thalia Bridgewood's stock down in Milledgeville), and kudzu vine, let

6

grow again after the war, crept over everything. Moths and mosquitoes pestered. The citizens of Rabun County's county seat wound their watches and drank Chatooga white lightning purposedly.

Kaye halted speculation. Sufficient unto the day, she assured herself, affirming one of the well-worn maxims her mother had employed—one, Kaye concluded, that, had Cordelia Bridgewood Wayfaring been able to make it her own, day by day, might have kept her back from the precipice overhanging Tallulah Gorge. Then she looked out over the Park, which, from her perch there on the highest rock in the Ramble, gave the impression of Cythera, and, with the boat lake stretching out to the south and west in a boomerang curve, of voyages thereto and of returns. "Make voyages, attempt them; there's nothing else!" her vehement dramatist mentor had charged. She thought of Ariadne. Ariadne on Naxos. Ariadne, the labyrinth guide.

She sneezed four times. The sun had disappeared behind a cloud. She thought, I've got more time. Then, looking up, she saw the Olympian figure of Orphrey Whither, looking like Bacchus, blocking the sun's rays in the west and the entire view of the Dakota Apartments (where Kaye had been installed, for the picture's term, in a gable in Hyperion Productions' New York pied-à-terre).

Kaye had decided long since that whenever she considered this O.W.—having summoned him for conversation in the daytime, or yakking on the telephone with him on a restless night—she considered him in terms of cubits rather than weights and measures such as feet, inches, pounds, stone, meters, or kilos. Orphrey Whither could glower; so he did. Kaye counseled herself: Men are not gods.

7

"May one know what you're up to this time, Miss Wayfaring, and for how long these meditations are like to last?" The Corkonian growl sounded, she thought, like something from out of a cave or up from a well, or like oracular sap gushing forth from some Druidic oak.

"Giving myself a piece of my mind, such as it is," she countered, working her own variation of the Thalia Bridgewood contralto.

"Actors!"

"I'm an actress."

"Don't quibble."

"It isn't a quibble, it's a tenet of meditation. And anyway, what do you care what-old-how I'm using this afternoon to get at this part? You're only the director."

"This is insupportable."

"Not in good light. Orphrey, you don't begin to terrify me. Candace does, *Avenged* does, but you do not. Sorry, old soak."

"I could replace you: you realize that."

"You know," Kaye replied to her tormentor, "you'd probably be eerily compelling as Candace, wearing Wayfaring's old hair."

"You aren't mildly funny."

"That's funny—*you* are a regular riot."

"How dare you go on like this!"

"I could go on like this all day. It's terribly relaxing, and it's what I did best at school."

"I cannot, and will not, bear it."

"I won't keep you much longer. But listen, Mister, do yourself a favor. No more whistles. I don't answer to a toot."

Orphrey Whither turned away. He pounded down the

8

scaffold steps leading from the rock to the glade. The Ramble's shadows lengthened.

Kaye Wayfaring considered the sweat of endeavor. Phrases, facts, fancies, options. Shadow aspects, libidinal commitment. Free-floating anxiety. Feeling edgy of an afternoon in fall. Phase-specific turmoil states. All this nervous bravado. An open declaration. Passions. Choices. The bottom line. Ariadne occupied, spinning threads. I'm obviously frantic, she advised herself severely. What must I do?

The light continued failing. She voiced her performance koan. *"The way out is the way in."*

Kaye Wayfaring set out to explore creation. She stalked the Ramble the way she once had stalked Warwoman Dell, like some predator, all the while considering, and all the while, as well, singing measuredly, sotto voce, the aria *"Che farò senza Euridice,"* from Gluck's *Orfeo ed Euridice.* She fancied it best sung, for her express purposes, in English, the way Kathleen Ferrier had sung it on records and the very way Mawrdew Czgowchwz (pronounced "Gorgeous"), oltrano, had sung it when—when she (Kaye) had been a drama student at Yale and the diva had arrived one evening in October to give a recital at Woolsey Hall. Thus Wayfaring, rambling, sang:

> *What is life to me without thee,*
> *What is life when thou art dead . . .*

Candace, hell-bent on revenge. The motive: thwarted passion. Very much the same old story, Kaye thought, decidedly worth telling one more time. Stalking, she improvised a riff on the *"Che farò. . . ."*

> *What is life when thou art dead*
> *To me and yet still live,*
> *Still laugh, still plunder,*
> *At liberty . . .*

Candace is avenged by arranging a marriage. A good one, that, thought Kaye, who had never married. She had loved, lost, loved, managed, loved, survived, loved, and stopped. Yet not necessarily. Kaye thought it through, and asked herself: Who wrote the very first torch song?

What is life when thou art dead?

The Ramble's tangled byways offered Kaye opportunity for exercise and for contemplation. A serviceable glamour —that's what I've hawked, she told herself, turning grouchy, feeling bruised, annoyed at the way branches would now and again protrude, like pointing fingers.

Candace plots, succeeds, avenges, all to no good, to no success. *Avenged,* a remake. So—so what: so was *The Letter.*

If I don't kill you, who will?

Good God, where did that one bubble up from? That tag line from *Way Station,* the film for which she had won her second Academy nomination. (Lost it that year, too, to another, lesser actress.) But on: press on. The Ramble's explosive foliage gave little solace.

What is life to me without me?

I, I, me, me, I, me, I. Oh, that one: her. Not now, not now. Have her call back. Wait, no, don't. Tell her not to call us: we'll call her.

She advanced, made progress. A rider on horseback passed over a bridge ahead.

That's what I should be doing. Look at him: that's the way to sit a horse. Has anybody ever told that boy he looks like something out of the *Arabian Nights?*

Even as she remarked upon him, the gallant rider was tossed off his mount and rolled partway down the hill, ending up, as Kaye quickly made for him to offer assistance, at her feet, stunned and abashed.

"Are you O.K.?" she asked, looking worried. "That fall looked like some kind of circus stunt."

"That was no stunt. I guess he recognized you and decided to present me this way. He has a sense of humor."

"Like certain press agents," she said, as he stood and brushed himself off.

"You don't remember me. I guess I really don't know why you should."

"Well, I'll certainly never forget you after this. Who are you?"

"Jacob Beltane, the younger son of Mawrdew Czgowchwz."

"Jacob—but you're all grown up!"

"Under the circumstances, that's very kind of you to say."

"I've been thinking of your mother on and off all afternoon."

"My mother has been thinking about you. That's why I'm here. Take this."

As Jacob Beltane the younger handed Kaye Wayfaring the letter his mother had entrusted to him, the receptor took the cavalier in.

"You've certainly come up tall. Presumably your brother has, too."

Kaye looked at the envelope, addressed in Mawrdew Czgowchwz's handwriting, and then back at the son.

This could be the missing link. Suppose instead of feeding all that rage into the brain's black hole, she sees this face. Look at that face. It's her: it's Mawrdew Czgowchwz:

the hair, the eyes. It's the fabulous father: the nose, the mouth. The way Jacob Beltane glowered on the old Met stage that winter in *Nosferatu*. Suppose she fixates on this creature's face—Nosferatu, before the fall. Could I get him to come around? This is a job for Mae West. My people could talk to his people. He's talking. . . .

"I told my mother I didn't think this was such a hot idea, but she insisted."

"She's a commanding person. Could you please tell her I'm thinking of her?"

"Will do." He was standing very tall. "Uh, good luck on this picture."

Throwing her head back, she indicated the general direction of the *Avenged* set. "This picture may take a while."

"Yes, so I hear."

"Perhaps you'd care to call again and cheer things along?"

"No, you're working. I know how you work. I worked with you once. I'd be in the way, and hate it."

"Do you write scripts?"

"You're teasing me. You teased us mercilessly."

"You were boys. I just had to. It was the drill."

"I'd better go. I'll come back some afternoon, but you must feel free to throw me off the set."

As JACOB BELTANE rode back over the bridge, Kaye remembered an incident involving her long-dead, long-mourned cousin Gabriel Wayfaring Bridgewood—an encounter in a violent summer storm back in Clayton. Thunder, lightning, wind, and rain: a tempest. She had sat the whole show out on the veranda roof. Afterward, when a sickle moon came up, Gabriel, older by two signs in the zodiac, the family stunner, a secret love, had approached her.

"Got a smoke, cuz?"

"They're wet."

"So are you, in point of fact."

"Why don't you go take a walk?"

"I was just trying to act like a friendly kissin' cousin."

"You want to get friendly, go find a dry cigarette."

"Diana Kaye, I will admit that if there's hot stuff around, you are some of it, but that does not give you any call to go around acting like such a ring-tail bitch. Don't you go to the picture show? It is the nice girls, like Tammy, that flourish."

"Look, this is *my* roof. Get lost."

"Tell me why you are this way."

"I live here—this is *my* roof."

" 'People who live for themselves are generally left to themselves.' Ever hear that? It's a line from a play. You mean to be an actress? Go look it up."

Dissolve, wipe. A new instant, another time. Kaye Wayfaring seeking, delving. Wanting out, occasionally: out of histrionic guile.

Do wash the ink off your hands.

Don't try to get too much in.

There is weight, and there is clutter: distinguish them, distinguish them.

The way out is the way in.

These had been the four best directives offered by the exacting Miss C.W., Kaye's teacher at Yale. Kaye, in improvisation, would talk on and on: "I've got a fat trap, that's what. I should shut up, I know I should, but there are times when I cannot think of a single thing not to say." Miss C.W. would remonstrate, "Do wash the ink off your hands."

Kaye Wayfaring, two-time Oscar nominee, star (who never wore anybody else's old hair), wondered. How long would the luck hold out? When the descent? When would it end? How fast, how soon? A trashy inquisition: she decided to forbear. Better to go down hailing a taxi than to end it all in some back row looking at Kaye Wayfaring (in *Avenged*).

On her first day in New York City, she had been invited to a Village party, just off Seventh Avenue, south of Sheridan Square. She had accepted; she had attended. She had become the sudden, spectacular rage. Just then, in the Ramble, remembering, she fetched it back.

She had been sitting at an open window, high up, south of Sheridan Square, and talking to herself. "I am a fragile vixen, and I prefer the dawn to the day" (a ghastly line from some Yale vehicle). "I'm naked," she'd called out the window. She saw out and she saw in.

They were strewn about the floor, the rest, all victims, all snoring. She had scribbled a note on the back of some stern manifesto and sent it sailing, folded into an origami airplane, down toward Seventh Avenue: "Two Schlitz and a pack of Luckies. Bless you.—Abandoned in 13-G." The note never made it to the avenue. It caught a crosswind, then a tailwind, and flew off toward the Midwest. She laughed; she rose. She looked about the room and she saw a microphone on a throw pillow. The cassette recorder sat there on the floor, with a quantity of her madness spooled on it, and most probably vaster quantities of the others'. She rewound the cassette and sat listening to the playback.

Snorers tossed and stirred from time to time. She listened to the section where someone had begged them all to join hands and hold their breaths, and then *hummmmm.* She listened to humming, then to silence, then to her own hysterical laughter. Then to slamming doors. (Somebody exiting, enraged.) Then she decided to hear no more.

Kaye decided it was high time to head back, all told. Enough of reminiscence. From such deliberate delving, from such a determined, willing plunge, one might develop, on the way up to the surface, to what is casually termed the present, a severe case of the bends. Miss Wayfaring sallied forth, like Mrs. Millamant, in full sail.

Here she comes back, she advised creation. Creation, entirely pleased, welcomed her at sundown. The way the last rays available from the sun setting in the west splashed her in vermilion—momentary raiment, all filmable, as halos briefly are—caused her to gleam. Her flaring, involved radiance matched creation's resources. She resembled some swan gliding along on a millrace. Her arching neck, thrust out in the very way she had determined, ages ago, it ought to thrust, signaled the very Kaye Wayfaring, voyaging to Cythera and back. She planned ahead. She had always specialized in fast, fabulous results, achieved while sailing through the lengths of fast, fabulous afternoons. Suddenly she had begun to question them all, the way she had begun to question the difference, for example, between "self-serving" (not nice) and "Help yourself" (fine). Was she as good as could be? Why did she suffer so from ill-defined predilective disorders? When would she make up her mind—in the cold, clear light of dawn?

Why the gods above me, who must be in the know . . .
How can I get along now . . .

Others find peace of mind in pretending . . .
What is life to me without thee . . .

Had it all been said, all done? Kaye recalled talking back to one self-styled wise old fool years before and insisting, "It may have all been said before, but not to me." The old fool had nodded gravely.

Kaye Wayfaring broke her defiant, thoroughbred stride. She sauntered; she relaxed; she calmed herself.

She opened the letter from Mawrdew Czgowchwz and began to read.

BACK on the set, Orphrey Whither had set about bullying Patrick More, the leading man. They stepped aside as gaffers adjusted apparatus. Miss Wayfaring crossed, nodding, to her trailer. Moments passed. The scene between Candace and Drew, the dupe, was set to roll at the cascade. Orphrey Whither seized control. "Overture and beginners!" he bellowed.

Jameson O'Maurigan had written in the original treatment: "Moments, events implode, all shaping *Avenged*. Haunting disembodied voices of the eternal New York night, consoling and menacing, counterpoint Candace's seizure. They are all matched to the faces of nameless lovers, careless assassins, on which collection, from shot to shot, is superimposed the furious face of Kaye Wayfaring, as Candace, determined to be avenged—her face set against the New York skyline. Face and skyline: twin emblems of the city as woman and as dream."

Playing the scene, Kaye, weaving, sinuous, reached out. She whispered; she grasped; she leaped; she plunged again. She became an avenger.

Orphrey Whither, holding a two-shot, quaked. This was a moment he'd dreamed he might capture on film one day: the wail of the city, endlessly dreaming itself. . . .

"Cut!"

"Will that do, Mister Whither?"

"That will suffice, Miss Wayfaring. Take ten."

"I'll take a dozen. Will that *do?*"

"It was a perfect take, and, what's more, you know it was. Now go and congratulate yourself."

"I owe it all to my director."

"Get lost."

"I've been lost."

They all took ten, and parted. Kaye took a recess in her trailer and read the Mawrdew Czgowchwz letter a second time. Then it was time for the long Wayfaring solo.

She exited and strode to her mark. All right, Wayfaring, she ordered herself. Navigate. She knew what she meant to do. She thought she just might at that. She thought she might just as well. She lit one of her necessary Luckies, took a puff, and stamped it out, letting go, as the bell rang for her to commence.

In the elaborate tracking sequence set to roll, Candace was to cross out of the Ramble and over the boat-lake bridge, and then, after a cut to the top of the stone staircase leading down to Bethesda Fountain, lope at a purposed, anguished pace into hell—the ruined piazza. One shot was to be held so that her feet, legs, torso, and face would pass in vertical review, revealing the woman hounded down by torment, driven to distraction at the reflecting pool over which an anonymous angel, whose name, Kaye had decided, was Victory, stands adamant sentinel: Candace fleeing the camera, her accuser. As Kaye Wayfaring progressed, light poured down on her from arc-lamp sources above, while the crane-mounted Panavision cameras rolled slowly alongside. One camera, its lens set to zoom when required, moved backward on a car some fair distance in front of her. Faces of onlookers bobbed back and forth from up on the rocks, floating in her field of vision like odd carnival balloons.

It was a long and terrifying walk. Freed from wordage, no longer a talking woman at all, she became gesture unbound, expanding, toiling—the very Kaye Wayfaring.

Jameson O'Maurigan scanned the action from the rocks above, amazed, as the actress, glancing from side to side time and again (enacting Candace seeking assistance from infernal gods), seemed to recognize a face, a presence here and there in the October dusk. "What a show! What's she up to?" the poet blurted out. The next morning's rushes would certainly present evidence of obsession. What an oracular performer Kaye Wayfaring had become. What abandon; what calculation.

Kaye Wayfaring, voyager. She'd set her way; now she progressed. Replaying the day, the week, the life, she altered expression rapidly, time and again. She was certain and she was correct.

What a way to live a life.

Here were stairs: no halting whatever. Like a deer trapped in headlights' glare on a country road back home in the shooting season, she, startled, surrendered. She looked across at the Dakota. *The way out is the way in.*

She stood dead still for a moment on her mark at the top of the stone steps. Orphrey and Victory beckoned from below. Blindly, she began the stumbling descent. Cameras positioned below whirred. Down she fled. Her face became the face of Death's own head. She looked again across toward the Dakota. It was not there.

She hit bottom. Raising her arms slowly, Kaye Wayfaring flung her body down at the Bethesda Fountain's stone-rimmed basin. Then she leaned forward, looking into the reflecting pool.

Orphrey Whither shouted, "Cut!"

Such was the work of that day.

THE SCAN OF
ILLYRIA

THE VIEW from the windmill's topmost window, a layered pattern—the grounds, the dunes, the beach, and the Atlantic—encouraged the spectator. On the croquet lawn, below, seats had been arranged for the evening's play: willow armchairs and bentwood rockers in the parterre, at ten dollars; folding canvas chairs with round cushions in the orchestra, at seven; two tiers of bleacher benches, loge and balcony, at four and three. To the left, beneath the window, apprentices crossed back and forth over the stage, dressing the set; to the right, members of the audience ambled through the coppice of silver birches and took snapshots of the lily pond, the gardens, the windmill, and the gray gambrel-roofed house. A party of children had grouped around the Shetland pony. An actor suited in motley, with cap and bells, holding a red-and-white-striped baton to which a hook-nosed fool's head had been affixed, sat cross-legged on the fulcrum of a seesaw, guarding four riders, two perched on each curved, chair-backed end. To the spectator in the summer-evening twilight, the dunes' configuration appeared first as settled as the rock cliffs of Tintagel, then as restive as the rims of Etna and Vesuvius. On the beach, workers mounted fireworks cartridges on slender scaffolding anchored with hawsers to sand buggies. The Atlantic looked rehearsed.

Kaye Wayfaring turned from the window and stared into the mirror. The mirror, studded with glowing bulbs and wreathed in telegrams, reflected the cheval glass set up against the wall opposite, creating the endless-passage effect she'd favored since childhood. She scanned her face, reiterated to the vanishing point. Without makeup, masked in egg white, the face resembled something archaic, unearthed from Pompeii. ("A good hat face," Kaye Wayfaring would grant, when talking business.) The portable oven timer's bell sounded; the setting interval was up. She mugged a yawn, and the egg white cracked into a webbed veil. (" 'I look like an old, peeled wall.' " She remembered another's part in another play, elsewhere. I may look like this for real one day, she thought.) Dipping a sponge into a bowl of warm seltzer on the dressing-room table, she began to remove the mask, preoccupied still with the previous night's dream, a masterpiece.

The dreamer stood on the back veranda alone, watching the summer-evening festivities. The performance had ended. The figures had cleared the folding chairs. In the light of multicolored Japanese lanterns, couples were dancing the foxtrot to postwar hits from 78s spinning on the Victrola. . . .

"One hour, Miss Wayfaring!" an excited voice called out from below.

The ship's clock over the mirror struck eight bells. She reset the timer to forty-nine minutes and switched the cassette recorder to Playback. She would listen to her words again, and stop and start and wait for the last call to come.

She heard the sound of her own voice reciting in a flat, uninflected tone.

What country, friends, is this?

Her mother had accused her of untoward love for the sound of her own voice. Who could love the sound of this? But it was the way in.

The Scan of Illyria

And what should I do in Illyria?
My brother he is in Elysium.

She listened to the shipwrecked Viola's exalted utterance, dialogue running fluidly, without cues, in this disembodied voice, her own yet foreign (accompanied by "that short, sweet phrase in F-sharp" she had asked her stalwart friend Tristan Beltane, guitarist and composer, to repeat again and again as she recited into the microphone), lapping evenly like waves at ebb tide on the calm evening of this Fourth of July, nineteen seventy-nine.

She heard the moan of airplane engines. Turning to look out the window again, she saw the white Phaeton cross in the sky from left to right, transporting its cargo of canned footage—the conclusion of *Avenged*—back to the film lab in New York. Handle with Care/This Side Up, Kaye Wayfaring directed. She remembered Marilyn Monroe in *Don't Bother to Knock*, desolate in a hotel room, pulling the venetian blinds open and shut, signaling her phantom pilot. From the plane's tail a banner trailed, its legend painted in Day-Glo vermilion, against the violet, gray, and lime-green sky: "Live Theatre Tonight! *Twelfth Night* at Nonsuch Stix!"

Turning back to the mirror to begin, she smoothed on a base of natural tan.

Mine own escape unfoldeth to my hope.

She took up the shading and the Cover-Me under-eye cream.

Conceal me what I am, and be my aid
For such disguise as haply shall become
The form of my intent.

25

The plane had passed. The hammering sounds and the ticking of the oven timer continued. Drowning out Viola's words, she intoned, "She saw Esau sitting on a seesaw. Esau seashore, seesaw was . . ." She hummed a low ommmmmm, filling her ears with the sound of engines again.

ON THE way out, the white custom-built Phaeton aircraft had cruised at an altitude of thirty-four hundred feet, at a speed of one hundred and sixty knots, on a due-easterly course over Flushing, Manhasset, Westbury, Oyster Bay, Cold Spring Harbor, Northport, and Lake Ronkonkoma, approaching Great Peconic Bay and the South Fork of Long Island. Off to the right, Kaye Wayfaring saw fishing boats in Great South Bay, and along the shoreline inter-locking polygonal webs of suburban housing units, shopping malls, narrow, curving streets, and straight, wide highways thronged with traffic—a complex in which no separate villages or towns could be made out. She decided it was all called Babylon.

Kaye drooped into a restless, wakeful doze. Points of light, reflecting incessantly off the calm Atlantic, kept her partly aware, beguiling her like familiar voices ascending in chromatic scales. The Phaeton's engines whirred. Her fellow-passengers—Orphrey Whither, the director of *Avenged*, and Patrick More, leading man—and the pilot, scripter Jameson O'Maurigan, chatted up front as if they were all out motoring in a tourer along some parkway down on the surface of the earth. Flying so high with three guys in the sky, then landing in paradise. (Orphrey and Jameson had promised her: paradise.) Kaye's memory,

winging, replayed: stranger in paradise, stairway to paradise (top hats and canes), the Paradise Mountain Drive-In
in Clayton, Georgia. *What* were paradise enow?

The picture, *Avenged*, was all but completed. Jameson
had written four variant endings, and Orphrey had decided
to shoot each one of them. The wonted collaborators called
them the earth/air/water/fire endings. One thing about
Avenged was certain: it would finish near, at, or in the
Atlantic. So may we all, Kaye Wayfaring thought. Now,
now, now, now! she advised herself, remembering her
mother: "You calm yourself, Miss. You are wildly dis-
tracted by the future!"

"Investing in past futures," she had been told by some
sage, "was the key to home.

The Phaeton drifted over Great Peconic Bay; then it
tilted, veering right, looping into the descent. Kaye, terrified of landings, lighted another Lucky Strike, telling
herself an actress never whimpers. Remember something
more, something from school. She looked through the
smoke, out the window, as the Phaeton hovered over the
terrain. Remember . . . *Illyria*. The ground drew close as
she gazed. She remembered *The Scan of Illyria*.

In her Yale Drama days a young Shakespearean scholar
called Daniel Mullein had come up from the University of
Virginia to stay one academic year at Jonathan Edwards
College and had given a set of lectures called *The Scan of
Illyria*. Kaye had been cast as Viola for the end-term
Twelfth Night, and her best friend, Jenn, as Olivia. The
avid scholar had spoken of Illyria as mise-en-scène, as mi-
lieu, as realm, and as idea (formal, efficient, exemplary,
final), enlightening the actress, who had spent half a year
on assigned "life walks" observing citizens: Miss Prism

("Young women are green!") on the Green; all three sisters
on one winter afternoon; Blanche, wandering down College Street, all elsewhere eyes and firm purpose ("Sometimes there's God, so quickly!"); and Goneril and Regan
yakking at Pegnataro's ("Whaddya makin', Roe?" "I'm
makin' *scungils*"). It was all new. Sense-memory, the intersecting circles, shtick, and the directives of her teacher,
Miss C.W. ("No good art ever came out of a glamour."
"Take the whole thing down to one.") Kaye had approached Daniel Mullein after the lecture. "I think I know
what to do." The scholar had attended the performance of
Twelfth Night, had approved, and had returned to Char-
lottesville.

She felt a jolt and cried out. The others shouted back to
reassure her. The Phaeton had landed. As it taxied along,
Illyria welcomed them.

"THAT was a month ago," Kaye said out loud.

> *I pray you, tell me if this be the lady of the house, for
> I never saw her: I would be loath to cast away my speech;
> for, besides that it is excellently well penned, I have taken
> great pains to con it.*

"Truer words you don't hear on a Sunday."

THEY had passed through the small country airport's white
clapboard terminal and, led by Orphrey Whither, headed
along the gravel path toward a row of stately elms shading
the entrance gate. Kaye took a deep breath of air. She

smelled honeysuckle, dogwood, bougainvillea, and the sea. Parked at the gate, motor running, stood a Pontiac station wagon with wood-paneled doors and running boards. At the open front door on the driver's side, wearing a classic straw picture hat with the brim turned up in front, aviator sunglasses, a flowing white smock, and spectator pumps, the fairest woman Kaye had ever seen stood waving a smoking cigarette, beckoning the party, her houseguests.

Orphrey, with executive finesse, supervised the introductions. "Pat I know you know of old, and the O'Maurigan personage. This is Kaye Wayfaring. Miss Wayfaring, meet Mrs. Boadicea Tillinghast—Till to her friends."

"Hello," said Kaye. "Thanks for having us all out."

"Couldn't be more attractive. Welcome to Stix Landing, the end of the line. Get in. You collection sit in back."

No Sunday traffic clogged the back road to the Tillinghast estate. No vehicle approached or overtook the slowly moving station wagon for more than a quarter of an hour, during which time Till talked without pause. Kaye listened attentively, concurrently aware of a sudden, sharp attack of hunger. She asked herself simply, relieved to be in the absolute present, What is life but gossip and nutrition?

Boadicea Tillinghast. Kell moniker. Kaye recalled an old Wayfaring family story. In the seventh month of her mother's pregnancy, while the family was summering at Sea Island, young Jackson Bridgewood the Fourth, the firstborn, had been asked what he thought his new brother or sister might be given for a name. "If it's a girl, call it Sponge."

"Town must be hell," gasped Till. "Well, you can cool off out here."

Kaye nodded, lighting up another Lucky Strike. Cool off, finishing *Avenged?*

"It's hard work trying to plan," Till said. "It all ends up a string—a rope—of tangled contingencies. Stock footage, back projection. Last summer I penciled in so many sequences, orchestrated such Byzantine routines—brunches, dinners, cocktails, and complex floor shows—that in the end I just fled. I said, 'That deck out there will cave in.' I'd overheard one kindly neighbor tell another, 'Another summer featuring one Tillinghastly charade after another.' I said, 'That one is so right.' That's when I flew the coop, flew up to Manitoy, vowed nevermore. Went out to lunch. Came back in October, when the coast was clear. Hideous long, wet winter. Wind-chill factors, flat-out grim, illegitimate days. Tomorrow seemed more than ever a truly impossible day to locate. Don't miss those rhododendrons. Each day, each day. Have you tasted wild beach plums? They're yet to come. Perhaps you will stay on after *Avenged.* One life, one day at a time. Nineteen seventy-nine is different; every sentient being is aware of it."

At Nonsuch Stix, over a festive meal of artichokes, seviche, tabouli, and shadberry fool, Boadicea Tillinghast continued her reminiscences.

"Then, when the ground broke in the January thaw—midwinter spring, snowdrops, mist—we all ran off on a dig. Turned up all kinds of evocative props, whole pails of them. Don't have a clue what any of it is, but it's all authentic. Rain for whole long weeks on end. Easter was not amusing—muddy, very muddy. Lots of damage to the dunes. May's been a lark, and now you."

As Kaye Wayfaring relaxed, sipping icy Moët, the host interrogated the three men on New York and *Avenged.*

Orphrey Whither spoke with severe relish and mock dismay of spiraling production costs, weather conditions, the treacherous antics of industry zombies, and the bankability of the leading lady. Jameson O'Maurigan and Patrick More dwelled wistfully on the more metaphysical aspects of the total picture, the world picture of which the motion picture *Avenged* was for Jameson the emblem, and for Patrick a good job of work. The sun had begun to set. Kaye Wayfaring stood up. "I'm for a walk on the beach."

"Good, let me point the way. You go off wandering. I'll bandy remarks with the committee."

Walking westward in twilight, at low tide, Kaye set about framing her particular complaint. She told herself she did not feel that swell.

Now, cut that out. Look at you. Just *look* at you!

It won't work, not this time, no.

Positively gorgeous. Echt. The truth's the truth.

The truth is old, fat, bald, and ugly. I don't think I'm such a much.

She strode a way, then sat down. Once, at Sea Island, her brother and his cohorts, playing conquistador, had buried her up to her neck in a back dune, and stalked away down to the surf, leaving her like Ariadne, Kaye's pet mythological frail, ditched on some rock pile in the middle of nowhere, abandoned by that double-crosser she'd saved from extinction in the dark underground. She'd played the fool.

I'll get this out of me yet.

Removing her old kimono, she waded boldly into the freezing cold Atlantic at seven-forty in the evening. Buoyed by the swell of a wave, she looked back at the garment draped over a length of driftwood, suggesting the form of a lounger.

Having a fabulous time? Life here is said to be idyllic. They go about merrily digging up the past and wearing it. And what would they all say if word leaked out that she's in the habit of talking to her clothing? Jung talked to his pots and pans—so what? She rode a high wave, turned, and looked at the horizon. How could Jackson have drowned, the fool? He never trusted a soul. Then he drowned. She turned to look back to shore. In the failing light, the kimono seemed to be Ariadne.

Ospreys circled overhead, screeching, disrupting, the way the gulls had the day Jack drowned. A wave hit from behind, tumbling her into the shoals. She pushed ashore, trembling. No, I am not an osprey.

Walking back, she focused her gaze on the gray house and the windmill. Nonsuch Stix. Ought to be called something *wyck*—Tillwyck. She thought of the place she might one year own. Kaywyck, Waywyck, Farewyck? She and her brother had declared themselves twin satraps of an entire plantation village, Wayfaring-upon-Amazon. They had assumed the identities of Sheena and Jack Wayfaring, the Swamp Fox; of She-Who-Must-Be-Obeyed-and-Adored and J. B. Wayfaring, the Scourge of the Jungle. In the back yard's one tall oak they had made a tree house out of willow branches and timber from a disused still. Jackson Bridgewood hated cars: their polis was entirely maritime, like Venezia. Coracles, sampans, barges, junks—they would own and run them all. They might or might not encourage tourism. They would surely entertain and perform masques.

She found Till and the men playing Mille Bornes while looking at the Indianapolis 500 on television. Moments later, smoking idly, she told herself: Much like watching paint dry on a barn wall.

32

. . .

PAINT dry fast cars dead men tell no tales but ours.

> *Make me a willow cabin at your gate,*
> *And call upon my soul within the house;*
> *Write loyal cantons of contemnèd love,*
> *And sing them loud even in the dead of night.*

Miss Wayfaring concentrated on painting her face. Eyebrow pencil, wet bark; eyeshadow, cream taupe, accents in teal and emerald rain, dusted over then with translucent powder.

> *My father had a daughter lov'd a man,*
> *As it might be, perhaps, were I a woman,*
> *I should your lordship. . . .*
> *I am all the daughters of my father's house,*
> *And all the brothers too; and yet I know not.*

They've been dead for years and years. Promised myself to stay off the horn this last month, and I did. Contending with the fearful black-cord disease. Even left the worn black book in the wall safe at the Dakota, stashed away with the old letters, the snapshots, and the charm bracelet. The letter from Mawrdew Czgowchwz is still sealed in the tunnel wall for good luck, and the diary my mother left behind is still in the safe at the Bank of Clayton.

Jenn's here with me on the job, Jenn and her Tristan, magical plucker. Jacob, Tristan's twin, is somewhere—where?

What's become of Wayfaring? She's died in all her pictures. Doing a play again, wherein she survives. Dreamed

33

the opening-night nightmare on schedule—unprepared, no lines, undressed, bald as a bean. Audience of gorgons and burping warthogs clapping in tumbril 4/4. Every vortical detail, as Till did say. All the while, in waking life, friends provide the needed nourishment. Bouillon, herb tea, seltzer, rosemary for remembrance . . . no, that one drowned; right church, wrong pew. Be staunch. Here she is, sittin' up, takin' nou'shment. I loved it when it was all new, before I had to get up at dawn to be found dead.

I warrant thou art a merry fellow, and carest for nothing.

ON THE morning after the party's arrival at Nonsuch Stix, overcast skies had held up shooting. Affronted, Orphrey Whither raged, seated magisterially in a fanback wicker chair at the edge of a potato field, underneath the stoutest elm on Further Lane. A few yards off, in the field, gaffers slouched on a worn Army blanket, shooting craps. The key grip and the Best Boy sat apart in camp chairs, sipping coffee, eating Danish, reading *Variety* and the *I Ching*.

In *Avenged*'s earth ending, the heroine, Candace, would perish when her Porsche 911SC swerved off the road at some lunatic speed and hit the sentinel elm head on. The setup for the aftermath—the vehicle crushed against the tree's trunk—had been examined at every angle and approved by the director. Required now for the shot to begin rolling in Panavision were the presence of sunlight, of the leading man, Patrick More, standing next to the tree, and of Candace's body shrouded in the wreckage by a broken branch in bright new leaf.

34

Kaye Wayfaring lay on a long aluminum table in her trailer, looking sideways out the door at the art and science of motion pictures, having been efficiently made up into a hideous, blood-soaked quantum of torn flesh and shattered bone. "This is what it is to act," she mumbled, sipping hot black coffee through a straw. Forbidden to move her jaw or part her lips, she gritted her teeth, glared fiercely, and hissed.

Jameson O'Maurigan, sitting opposite, spoke soothing words. "We'll have a swim, then eat cake, laugh, point fingers, and go flying nowhere and back."

I don't eat cake, she objected silently.

The sun came out. Kaye was wheeled to the wrecked Porsche, hoisted, deposited, arranged, and covered with the broken branch. Orphrey Whither approached her.

"One short take, Miss Wayfaring. Eyes open in death, no expression. Ready—roll!"

Kaye blanked. The sun struck her eyes and bathed her face, revealing her. She heard a voice from the past call out, "Don't look at the sun that way!" She held fast, counting seconds, seeing colored spheres gyrating in a white glare, until she heard her director call out, "Cut! That's a print!"

The actress emerged, alive. "Let me go swim this muck off." She headed with Jameson down the road to Rhubarb Beach, past scattered batches of onlookers—townspeople and holiday-makers eager for a glimpse of Kaye Wayfaring in the flesh. The *Avenged* crew, breaking, followed along behind. Orphrey Whither's chair was planted on top of the highest rise. He sat down to view this interim sequence.

Boadicea Tillinghast had telephoned Kip's Liquors and East End Delicatessen, and by noon four beach buggies had arrived, loaded with crates of chilled wine and platters of baroque eats.

Orphrey Whither picked up a bullhorn and aimed it at the surf. "Miss Wayfaring is requested on the set!"

Out beyond the breakers, Kaye turned to Jameson. "What on earth is he up to? You know, don't you?"

"What should I know? I just work here, same as you."

"You do, though—I know you do."

"Once I knew. Those were the days."

"What are those trucks? What's the game?"

"The old questions are the great questions."

"You know."

Orphrey Whither descended from his dune to meet her halfway down the beach. Tendering a knot of slipper orchids, he spoke a sotto-voce aside. "Give the citizens a smile, Miss Wayfaring. We're celebrating your birthday."

"You old twister, it isn't until Wednesday."

"All art is rearrangement."

"There won't be anybody here on Wednesday?"

"Nobody but us cousins. Come and be radiant and cut the cake."

SHE PASTED one long false eyelash onto her left eye. She reached for a rose from the cluster of thirteen opening up. "To the Wayf, from two fast friends," the white card read. They were a good pair, those two. It is not good for man to be alone, the poor, rambunctious item.

> *By innocence I swear, and by my youth,*
> *I have one heart, one bosom, and one truth,*
> *And that no woman has; nor never none*
> *Shall mistress be of it, save I alone.*

Never Candace, nor Viola.

She remembered her mother standing on the back veranda, gaily toasting empty space. "Here's to the men in our lives. The stinkuhs."

I resemble my mother. She looked at herself. Resemble? It's the same face. It looks at the world the same way.

JAMESON had taken Kaye flying, as he'd promised. The white Phaeton circled over the town, the beach, and the splendid estates.

Kaye, calmed, had nearly run out of remarks. "Nobody working down there."

"Oh, but they are. They all are," Jameson assured her, smiling. "It all looks as serene as Illyria from this height, but they're all at it down there. Absolutely everybody working on another play, picture, book, pot, song, dance, life. There are also farmers planting potatoes, fishermen out trawling, and the like."

"Too bad we don't get to meet the like in our great work."

"Look down there. See that long flat stretch? That's where they shot Valentino in *The Sheik.*"

I'm listening and learning, she told herself. Something about topography and cloud formations and obedience to flight patterns and magnetism relative to the North Pole. I'll get it bit by bit.

GOT THAT? Get her. They got her.

. . .

Upon landing, she was drafted, as is. Swept up and off in a chopper to a cliff near Montauk Light, she was stationed out on the edge and shot playing at choking to death in thin air.

That was the one that was fun, in a stark way. Dialogue with wind machine, do-re-mi-faaa, do-re-mi-faaa, do-re-mi-faaa . . . She died on G. Then came O.W.'s pat on the head. "Gemini is air; ruler, Mercury the messenger. A job well done, Miss Wayfaring." What was that great old line? "Well, darlings, if you *must* go, try to remember one only did it for the money."

Come and cart this one off in a good, tight net.

The first of the fireworks exploded, scoring the darkened sky in red, silver, and electric blue. Trailing white smoke lingered in a web of streaks outside the window. She looked at herself made up, then shut her eyes again. Why are we the way we are? Keep checking the facts, the prints, and the m.o. She sat still, eyes shut, practicing isometrics, looking through the old snapshots she had left locked in the wall safe on Central Park West. In the first, taken on her seventh birthday, she was alone, standing upright in outsize heels, looking staunch, wearing lipstick, holding a palmetto fan. On the back her father had written, "Born on Decoration Day—She's some swell decoration that's a fact." The matinée-idol lout. It's a wonder she didn't hit the big town deciding to call herself Decoration Wayfaring. In the second, she stood arm in arm with Jenn. She was costumed as the boy Cesario, in breeches and jerkin, her hair clipped, waved, and dyed coal black, her attitude colt swagger. On the back she had written, "Pray God defend me! A little thing would make me tell them how much I lack of a man."

> *I hate ingratitude more in a man*
> *Than lying, vainness, babbling drunkenness,*
> *Or any taint of vice whose strong corruption*
> *Inhabits our frail blood.*

The fireworks continued exploding.
It had rained the night before the water ending.

SHE HAD lain still, counting sovereign heads and snapshot faces. What to do to mulch dead kin? Within minutes in the darkness she realized sleep would fail to arrive. A warning stir, one she likened to a whisper, an aura, only soundless, lightless, came from nowhere knowable, from a lost reach. She sat up, switched on the light, and tried reading something in current events containing pertinent information on a subject to which aware citizens in a participatory democracy ought to direct their attention, but she could not. Then, smoking, hedging familiar panic, she slowly force-read from the beginning a recently issued as-told-to, remnants of the life of a legendary icon-firefly of the silent screen: the meteoric rise, the peak, the feasting; the amatory excess, the headlong descent, the penitential survival alone in a room—until the electric storm knocked out the lights and she lay listening to the thunder, trying not to see the old photographs again, or the photographs in the as-told-to's picture section, and failing.

An hour or so before dawn, she fell into that state of anguish in which mismatched words and images, shaping nothing genuine, besiege the mind, paralyzing intention: shouts, laughter, warnings, threats, unknown composite faces, architecture never built, varieties of grotesque vegetation. Then came enraged indictments from the past, coincident with gibberish dispatches from a future that does not exist but assures annihilation.

The storm ended, and she lay looking through the skylight, smoking. She heard her mother's voice calling from long ago, "Jackson, kindly inform yoah sistuh that when she is finished bein' mindless, supper's on the table and there's preparations foah tumorruh." She slept until eleven.

"Half-hour, Miss Wayfaring!" The ship's clock struck one bell.

> *Methinks his words do from such passion fly,*
> *That he believes himself; So do not I.*
> *Prove true, imagination, O, prove true,*
> *That I, dear brother, be now ta'en for you!*

She stood with Jameson on the beach, looking out at the Atlantic. "Now I don't want to do it."

"I know you don't."

"I'll do it, though. The thing is what it brings back. The only question there really is—the two-part one I'm never able to shake for any decent interval. How will I die? Will it hurt?"

"Kaye, don't."

"How do you dream this stuff up, all you who do?"

"I can't say I wish I knew."

"Well, cheer up—it's only a movie."

The scene bell rang. Kaye Wayfaring set off along the beach as the cameras tracked her from the front and from the side. In spite of the presence of collaborators, she had never felt more the sole perpetrator, never more isolated, more bereft. She made no attempt to seem or to act. She kept walking, feeling her hooded costume shrouding her completely. The surf beat in short, dull thumps. She looked straight into the camera—a thing she had never done. She blinked, opened her mouth as if to speak, then swerved and waded into the Atlantic. She turned her head, screamed, and disappeared beneath the waves.

Moments later she stood wrapped in a beach robe as Orphrey Whither approached.

"Don't ever ask me to do that kind of thing again."

"I think we have what we need."

"I'm glad of that."

SHE HAD assumed the face of Viola, yet Candace kept exploding. The fireworks flashed in quickening succession, each burst flung at the sky reminding Kaye of battles she'd been told of as a child—of cannons, war play, all the martial clamor in the name of Wayfaring and man's country, this U.S.A.

The apprentices had finished with the set. The light crew was running the opening storm sequence one last time. Suddenly, from directly beneath the window, Kaye heard familiar music—young maestro Tristan Beltane playing the F-sharp opening to his *Willow Cabin* suite, completed that same morning. The composer's dexterity and the intricate clarity of his musical statement invited her to attempt proving again what it might be to go on, to take on so.

> *In favor was my brother; and he went*
> *Still in this fashion, color, ornament,*
> *For him I imitate. O! if it prove,*
> *Tempests are kind, and salt waves fresh in love!*

How did this *Twelfth Night* come up? Who said what first, what next?

IN THE evening, after the water ending, Kaye Wayfaring had received a welcome visitor.

"You know I seldom get up here, and it's my favorite corner of all."

"It would be mine."

"Then you must stay on and on."

"Thank you, Till. I feel at home."

"*Avenged* is nearly finished."

"And it's all theirs. I have no opinion whatever of Wayfaring in it."

"Opinion is the fundament of all misery."

"I'll drink to that."

"And to success, notwithstanding."

"Success. Notwithstanding what?"

"Notwithstanding anything."

"Here's how."

"*Slainte.*"

The whiskey warmed the new friends as Boadicea Tillinghast expanded her text. "I mean, here we are, so let's. Let them say what they will. That sort of thing, you know?"

"Sure, what the hell."

"You said it."

Kaye felt enlivened by this civilized vaudevillian, the kind of striking woman forties comediennes cast as side-kicks played, who seemed to be in on some merrily exponential solution to woe itself.

"What I like to do up here is watch the sky pass over. Do you gaze?"

"Gaze?"

"Stars."

"Oh. No, I did as a child—or rather my brother did, pointing constellations out. The names were all important-sounding, resonant. But I never studied astronomy, no."

"Very comforting, celestial investigation."

"I must try it while I'm here."

"I highly recommend it."

"Here's to celestial investigation."

"And to success. And to Happy Birthday."

"Thank you again."

"The scheme tonight is moon conjunct Jupiter. Great expectations."

"There's a mercy."

"Talking of schemes, would you like to do a play?"

"Do a play. How?"

"To do a thing, one does it. Let's do it here."

"But the Council season is all set. I saw the signs."

"Oh, not with *them!*"

"Well then, with whom?"

"Well then with us."

"Us. You?"

"The Nonsuch Stix Repertory Company of Friends. We're really very good."

"I see. And where?"

"Oh, right here at Nonsuch Stix."

"Wait, now, let me see if I can envision all this."

"FIFTEEN minutes, Miss Wayfaring!"

She closed her eyes. What she saw first was another of the photographs—one she had taken herself, of her mother standing alone on the front veranda of the house in Clayton, Georgia. The large, dark eyes were shadowed under the wide brim of a white straw picture hat, but the other components of the smile—the mouth, the nose, and the set of the jaw—were clearly outlined. The smile, a stretched, snapshot smile, resembled an amusement-park-billboard grin. It was her mother's matinée smile; it read, "Everybody come in heuh to the festivities!"

Next she saw movement—figures rushing about. She ran past her mother, through the house, out into the back yard, where her mind's eye staked out a vantage, underneath the willow, which allowed a view through a tendril curtain: the old victory garden, the back veranda, and, to the left of the house, the tall oak and the tree house. A clothesline had been strung between the oak and the hickory at the property's north boundary, and a traverse curtain fashioned out of a surplus parachute and dozens of brass rings some dead Wayfaring had left in a steamer trunk (wrapped in a remnant of stars-and-bars bunting, with a note attached: "Won every one") had been hung to be drawn across the playing area. The figures were setting up folding chairs.

. . .

"But what if the deck caves in?"

Boadicea Tillinghast frowned. "We don't perform on the deck."

"Sorry."

"Nonsense. Glad you brought it up. Very important question indeed. We did not play last summer. I hit the road. Most appalling cowardice."

"And this summer?"

"We must atone. We must deliver again."

"You sound very serious."

"I am—very serious."

"And you think Wayfaring would fit in?"

"Well, she can act; I've seen her."

"Isn't she one of those picture people?"

"Oh, I've seen her on the stage—once, in *Twelfth Night.*"

Kaye laughed. "You came to Yale?"

"Oh, all the time. C.W. was a dear, particular friend."

"Was Wayfaring any good?"

"She had remarkable eyes. Still does, really."

"But could she talk?"

"She owned her words. She picked up her cues and flew."

"Kid on the run."

"There is a fierce need to replenish, to renew incessantly, keeping up appearances. You realize we're never supposed to stop."

"All I seem to do is stop."

"Stop, not finish?"

"Exactly. Fire ending tomorrow. *Avenged* over and out. Wayfaring left to go on."

. . .

WHERE was Till now? Making up herself, in another room, to go on. In the back yard of the star's mind the summer-evening festivities in Clayton progressed. (In Kaye's memory, Wayfaring revels never ended; she'd fled from them.) There she was, spotlighted in the tree house, costumed in parachute silk, enacting the wayward Guinevere.

There lingered Jackson Bridgewood Wayfaring the Fourth, in the scuppernong arbor.

THE OVEN timer sounded.

She'd slept on it, all of it, and here she was.

"Ten minutes, Miss Wayfaring!"

Ten minutes! My hair, my nails, my face! I must look a fright.

I do not. I look the part. Viola, not Candace. Candace has been extinguished. I remember exactly how.

Outside, the pinwheel production-number finish started. The room turned red, blue, more red. The smell of sulphur grew strong. Voices cheered the spectacle as Kaye sat still and heard her words.

> *He did me kindness, sir, drew on my side;*
> *But in conclusion put strange speech upon me:*
> *I know not what 'twas but distraction.*

THEY had dressed her in white batiste and blocked her seated at a long Directoire table in the loft of the disused Tillinghast barn, surrounded the area with mirrors, waited for the sunset, smashed the mirrors to pieces, ringed the set with stage-fire barrows, set them alight, and filmed Candace writing her last letters—to the man who had left her and to the world she would leave. Kaye, sitting, waiting for the take, wrote to Jenn and Tristan Beltane.

Dearest,

The latest in abreaction and accidie: she sits here draining herself of the stuff of life. (Looking alive, she'd compromise the image.) In this, the fire ending, she goes strenuously bonkers (dead around the irises) in the atelier, and flares to cinders in front of the mirrors she's just smashed. Vility, madness—snuffed out. So I need you quick out here. . . .

It's really very simple. We're going to do *Twelfth Night; or, What You Will* on the croquet lawn at Nonsuch Stix, with a complex of local stalwarts, to raise cash to renovate the meeting hall, repair the erosion suffered by the dunes, and save the elms from the Dutch blight. Plus we'll spread joy. (Candace is a killjoy; she is making Wayfaring nuts and sad.) Please say yes, here is the plan. . . .

THE LAST explosions illuminated the night sky.

> *And all those sayings will I over-swear,*
> *And all those swearings keep as true in soul*
> *As does that orbèd continent the fire*
> *That severs day from night.*

I never watched the fire-ending rushes.

The actor suited in motley crouched at the foot of the stage and set about beating an orotund parade drum softly as Tristan Beltane positioned himself upstage left and began strumming chords and runs. The audience was summoned. "Show time! Show time!"

Overhead, the moon had begun its Julian transit of Pluto, Uranus, and Neptune. Kaye closed the window, standing to one side to avoid being seen from below by the audience arriving at their seats. There were Whither, O'-Maurigan, and Boss Tillinghast, Yankee dreadnought, keeping tabs on the take. Boadicea, as Maria, wrongly costumed, looked like Rembrandt's Saskia as Flora the Walking Maypole. Through the turnstile passed this one, that one, and the other one. Famous faces, very nearly, nearly, not nearly. Moving mouths expressed opinions. One day they would all be right. They were all right then, in certain discrete situations. Life is a dream—it says so.

Who are those women Jameson's reaching toward that way? Lord, it's Mawrdew Czgowchwz, my idol and nemesis, and Jameson's aunt, the Countess Madge O'Meaghre Gautier—neither of them looking two days over forty-nine. Who's that coming in behind them? It's Halcyon Paranoy, with Chimère. That one. He'll be shooting the whole performance through some hidden periscope nostril camera, and I won't be able to prove a thing, or want him to stop, either.

I clawed my way to the top. No, I did not. I'm good, I'm kind. Or else this is not the top. Look at all those lovely paying customers. Get out and go to a play. Nineteen seventy-nine is different; every sentient being is aware of it. I'm having an opinion; it's the music. If I start to cry, what then? Dear God, let her not be swamped. She has a performance to give. She's never been a no-show. Let her go on, get off, go home—those whereabouts, wherever they next may be. Let me take this down to one.

"Curtain time, Miss Wayfaring!"

The door of the windmill's top room opened slowly. A voice below commanded, "Overture and beginners!" The sound of the parade drum beating in 4/4 time was augmented by the rattling of aluminum sheets to represent a storm. Then the opening cadence of *Willow Cabin,* in F-sharp, for krummhorn, sackbut, viol, and lute. Kaye Wayfaring descended, awake—left the rack to hit the deck.

Twelfth Night; or, What You Will had begun at Nonsuch Stix. Patrick More spoke to the instrumental ensemble:

> *If music be the food of love, play on;*
> *Give me excess of it, that, surfeiting,*
> *The appetite may sicken, and so die.*
> *That strain again! it had a dying fall . . .*

The waking dreamer took short, processional steps, concentrating on the path. She would reach her mark in just the time it took, charged with the outtake loop she'd dreamed the night before. Her late dream would take her to one.

The dreamer stood on the back veranda alone, watching the summer-evening festivities. The performance had ended; the figures had cleared the folding chairs. In the light of multi-colored Japanese lanterns, couples were dancing the foxtrot to postwar hits from 78s spinning on the Victrola. Lancelot, dressed down to Kilroy the Spectacular, had sped off in the Packard with his cronies. She waved goodbye to the Clayton dancers, who stopped all at once and, as the record needle stuck on an upbeat phrase, turned together in a phalanx and waved back as the Wayfaring house slipped from its moorings and drifted into the night. Her mother ran toward her, missing the sailing by seconds. She cried out, "Watch yourself, Miss Defiant!"

The dreamer turned and walked into the kitchen to find herself in the Grand Saloon of the R.M.S. Boadicea. *Couples uniformly dressed to the nines were dancing a hectic beguine across a mirrored parquet floor. The dreamer wove through them, swiveling, executing backbends with abandon. The dancing passengers encircled her, crooning:*

"Dream lover, put your arms around you . . ."

Two strangers accosted her, acting mock-ominous:

"I'm the woman without a shadow."

"I'm the man who knew too much."

She fled from the Grand Saloon, out onto the rear deck. The man and the woman called after her:

"That deck out there will cave in!"

She stood alone at the taffrail and watched the lights of imperial Manhattan recede until there was nothing to see in the darkness and nothing to hear but the voices of sailors below, singing an off-key chantey, the words of which were a catalogue of the clipper ship's sails. The rear deck was now the fo'c'sle.

> *Flying jib—jib—foremast stays'l*
> *Fores'l—fore lower tops'l*
> *Fore upper tops'l*
> *Fore t'gallants'l blow the man down.*

There was no wind, but the clipper ship moved forward, slicing through a glass-calm sea, bound south-southeast. Over the chantey's drone, the dreamer sang:

> *Blow the wind southerly, southerly southerly,*
> *Bring back my sweet bonny lover to me.*

There was no wind. A tempest rose in a dream instant. Lashed to the mast in a fierce icy rain, the dreamer underwent an ordeal of transformation. She became Odysseus. Sirens sang in multiple Kaye Wayfaring voices:

> *While far from heaven and thee*
> *I wander in a fragile bark*
> *O'er life's tempestuous sea . . .*
> *This way turn your bows,*
> *Moor and be merry . . .*
> *O bring back, O bring back,*
> *O bring back my bonny to me.*

Odysseus, male, despaired. The vessel sank. The voyager drowned. The night sea journey ended.

Kaye Wayfaring drifted at dawn, naked in a coracle. Soon the boat was washed onto a beach sloping down from a rise where a windmill overlooked the seacoast. A solitary figure stood there waiting, holding a cowled, rough-spun garment folded over one arm. The dreamer, wading through the shoals, arms at her sides, approached and addressed the stranger.

Kaye Wayfaring stood in the hot rose glow, turned, and spoke:

"What country, friends, is this?"

"This is Illyria, lady."

Something
Sensational
to Read
in the Train

"WELL, OUT with it," the *Variety* stringer demanded. "It's been in the can for over a year. What's he think it's going to do in there, improve with age? God knows, *we* don't. What's it look like, can you say?"

"It's awesome—very unique," the publicist replied.

"You got *your* check."

"No, I mean it. It should put Wayfaring back on top as the penultimate screen goddess. And, by the way, Whither shot the definitive new ending only last January."

"Wayfaring back on top. Well, if it doesn't, there's always religion. There's the legitimate *thea*tuh. She can revive Ibsen, Chekhov, Pirandello, and O'Neill on the Rialto. She can crap out in the straws every summer forever. She can do *tele*vision. It's a living."

"She's a dynamite actress," the unit publicist declared with fervency.

"That's a deep truth. She has also begun to assume the physical proportions of the legendary Marie Dressler. That's a bald fact."

"Care to order, gentlemen?"

"A martini, very dry, please, Claudia."

"The same."

"We're drinking to steady-cam."

"Drink to anything you like," answered Claudia, the barkeep, a witness, "as long as you voted. That's the important thing. Otherwise you have no right to agitate later."

"They took the vote away from publicists."

Moored together at the curve of the Neaport Bar, in

55

the landmark East Side Manitoy Hotel, the concerned pro-
fessionals endeavored to come to terms with Hyperion
Productions' motion picture *Avenged*, starring Kaye Wayfaring, directed by Orphrey Whither, set to premiere
that evening at the Metropolitan Opera House. Behind
them, and just at a level with their heads, encased in an
oblong teak-framed vitrine extending the length of the
snug bar's back wall, the diorama representing the harbor
of the bar's namesake town, Neaport, on the Massachusetts island of Manitoy, depicted for the moment a bright
nineteen-forty-seven July afternoon.

"I heard the shooting ratio was one to nineteen," offered
the stringer. "At least they talked him out of releasing the
opus in 3-D."

"Really." The unit publicist nodded, then shook his
head sideways. "They went with the Technicolor, but they
couldn't endorse the 3-D."

"A stereoscopic Wayfaring would be too much, even
considering her legendary bullet-proof angles."

"She's the greatest actress working in pictures."

"Also now a casualty. Clearly one of the walking
wounded."

"It took a lot out of her."

"She should get the Purple Heart!"

"She should get the Academy Award, hopefully."

"You said it— Don't spill any."

The weather behind the glass at Neaport changed at
once. A denizen of Broadway put a quarter in the Wur-
litzer jukebox and played Spike Jones's rendition of "Cocktails for Two." The conversation progressed.

"I remember very well," the *Variety* stringer announced, toasting the diorama. "Nineteen years ago this
coming summer. I crossed over to Manitoy in the pouring

56

rain to see the young Wayfaring play Stella in *A Streetcar Named Desire.* Nobody remembers the dame who played Blanche that summer. Nobody but me. Maybe that's why I come here."

"You mean because Claudia played Blanche du Bois."

"That summer on Manitoy—you guessed that."

"I haven't guessed anything since the Oscars. I lost. I got Claudia a pass for tonight. She thinks Wayfaring's the greatest living functionary currently before the battered public."

The veteran actress barkeep approached her customers. "Another round, gentlemen?"

"I've got to call the desk," the stringer said. "Remember when they used to call this town 'Fun City'? When I get back, let's all salute the past. And the future—the future of *Avenged.* Let's all do that."

He went to make the phone call.

"Claudia?" the publicist inquired, looking at Manitoy.

"What, hon?"

"You're a serious woman."

"I can be. You in trouble?"

"I am going to ask you to keep a secret which I feel I must share with one other human being besides God. Something you won't read in Gloria Gotham tomorrow on the subway to work. It's about Kaye Wayfaring."

"Subway? I take the elevator to work."

"Even so—even more so. You will read in the elevator the four-star review of *Avenged,* but you will not read this. I have just come here in a cab from Penn Station, where I picked up a single reservation, made in the name of Miss Artemis Grey, for a journey on the Nite-Owl Express to Route One twenty-eight—that's just outside of Boston."

"I know where on earth it is. I've gotten off at that stop

myself, to go—to go there." She pointed to the diorama, now featuring a sunset.

The unit publicist sighed. "Of course you did. Sorry, I have retention trouble. The secret is, Miss Artemis Grey—"

"Miss Artemis Grey is Kaye Wayfaring, and she's going to Manitoy to get away from *Avenged*. No promotional tour. There's almost certainly a man in the picture—in the actual picture."

"Claudia, are you psychic?"

"The guy who does her hair does mine."

"Cégèste is your hairdresser?"

"I paid my dues. There are particular services I still continue to require."

"So, who's the guy?"

"Ya got me."

The publicist paused, and said offhandedly, "Mawrdew Czgowchwz, another client of Cégèste's, is coming out of seclusion to attend the *Avenged* premiere."

After a markedly long pause, Claudia made a sweep with the bar cloth she was holding.

"All right, so *you* know what's going on and *I* know what's going on. I am still not dishing the situation."

"Just as well. My partner the newsman is coming back. It's between you and me and the folks at home on the island of Manitoy. Don't spill any."

"You said it."

KAYE WAYFARING, smoking, sat at a southeast gable window in the Dakota Apartments, overlooking Central Park. Blowing a set of four perfect smoke rings, one through another, she told herself: This is the window to throw it out of, lady.

She looked down at the Park and wondered when it would look like the Park again, no longer a location from *Avenged.* Perhaps when she'd finished with her business there tonight. She looked up at the sky, which made her think of the sea, as when the two, viewed in bright sunlight on a late spring afternoon, can seem the same. She thought of walking with Jameson along the beach on the South Fork, in between takes of the suicide-by-drowning sequence. She thought of walking along the beach at Tangent Point on the island of Manitoy with somebody else, someone she hardly knew.

Men and the sea; men landing; men behind cameras; men friends in need.

She stubbed out her Lucky Strike, and picked up the two books lying on the occasional table next to her comfortable chair. One was the moompix autobiography she'd held on to for over two years, and the other was the *I Ching.* The bookmark in the autobiography bore a legend, in Kaye Wayfaring's hand, copied out from the text: "Every actor has a natural animosity toward every other actor, present or absent, living or dead." (Plus which all the world's a stage, she told herself.) Many of the pages of the *I Ching* —which she had plied earlier that afternoon—were dog-eared and foxed with penciled annotation, some in her hand, some in others. The leaf she'd been working on directed: Lin. Approach. K'un Chen.

When there are things to do, one can become great. Hence there follows the hexagram of APPROACH. Approach means becoming great. . . .

APPROACH *has supreme success.*
Perseverance furthers.
When the eighth month comes,
There will be misfortune.

She told herself: There's too much information. Putting both books to one side on the window seat, she reached for one of what she had grown up calling her tablets, which the books had been stacked upon, opened it to a clean page, and wrote: *"La vida es sueño. Viven los que rien."*

The gala *Avenged* premiere. They're on their way to costume her and make her up. (The old question: You can dress her up, but can you take her out?)

On the whole, I'd much rather be getting ready to go out and hear Stretch Limo, Spotted Dick, Immediate Release, or Steroid.

Who am I? Where do I come from? What do I want? Where am I going?

Kaye Wayfaring, the actress. Clayton, GA, Los Angeles, CA, Yale School of Drama, and New York City. Another chance. To the Metropolitan Opera House. To the Tavern-on-the-Green. To the Ramble. Back here. To the Café des Artistes. To Penn Station. To Manitoy.

She put her pen down and glanced at the two books.

Why can't I sit quietly reading and clocking my future instead of cluttering up this page with impressions calculated to astonish mankind?

She wrote, "The seventies, long over . . . ," capped the pen and put it down, and looked out the window again, resisting the urge to smoke another cigarette. The appointed hour came; the bell rang. She sat still while the yeoman gaffer who had been Best Boy on *Avenged* answered it, and when the precise moment came for her to do so, she leaned sideways out of the chair, looked back, and drawled, "*Cégèste,* how lovely to see you. What have you decided to turn this flotsam into for tonight?"

Two men had walked into the room. Cégèste, removing his rings and handing them to his accomplice, grinned and tapped the crown of his bald skull four times.

"Miss Wayfaring, into what can one turn, all said and done—onez best, onez worst—the most perfectly realized woman in motion pictures?"

"Good question," Kaye Wayfaring nearly growled. "The Wrath of God? Death's Own Head? How about a slender woman again?"

"You're going into upset. Why do we not stick to essentials?"

"I like that approach; it's always authentic."

"A little *avoirdupois,* more or less—the fact remains you are the echt American love goddess."

"Somebody just walked over my grave. Easy on the back-combing."

"The merest *traipse.*"

"I like it—I'll endorse it."

The make-up and hairdressing process got under way.

"Miss Wayfaring, you are a gallant trouper."

"Cégèste, *why* must the show go on?"

"But where else would the show go?"

"Ah, that is clearly a metaphysical question. It has no relation to the facts of life as we know them—celebrity, amphetamine, cocaine, and world-round roller-coasters."

"I get no kick."

"You get your check."

"Miss Wayfaring, in the four decades I am in Show Business, but one other woman expresses herself to me like you do."

"Mawrdew Czgowchwz, oltrano, the definitive diva, my idol and nemesis, from whose home in Gramercy Park you have no doubt just come, as she is attending the *Avenged* premiere this evening."

"What nemesis?"

"As my mother would have answered, it's an expression —still, I have always wanted to sing Minnie in *La Fanciulla del West.*"

"This I would not put past you."

"Cégèste, I'm nearly forty."

"Bite your tongue, Miss Wayfaring," Cégèste, alarmed, cautioned, "or other tongues will wag!"

"Georgie knows how old I am. Keep it under your fedora, Puddin'-pie. Loose lips sink ships."

"I don't wear hats in the spring."

"Well, kindly don't let it hang out of your back pocket."

"Loyalty is my only idea of religion."

"You're both true blue, that's a fact. I kiss you both."

"Keep looking straight ahead, please—this is a delicate arrangement."

Out the window in the middle distance, she saw, or seemed to see, sitting in a rocker suspended in the eye of a tornado, her mother, the former Miss Cordelia ("Cora") Bridgewood, of Clayton and Atlanta, Georgia, holding a batch of curling papers in one hand, a curling iron in the other, and wearing an expression on her face that Kaye had learned to read as "Very funny, Miss Trouble." And to hear again the recitation of prescriptions and lengthy rules ("I do not use a Toni kit because, as is well known from advertisements circulated everywhere in tacky beauty parlors, Toni kits are meant for twins, and the Lord knows you are one of a kind, Miss!") intercut with quantities of antiphonal gossip ("That Peggy Marsh had that ole book about your great-great-gramma locked up in her closet . . .") interrupted in the telling always by one or more syncopated cut-to-the-bone dispatches ("What you're gonna *do* is *this* . . .") delivered over the phone on a routine afternoon. ("What I am busyin' myself with operatin' heuh is a psycho-analytical dis*pen*sary, Miss.") The figure rose from the chair as the tornado stilled. ("Now you should come to understand this right off the bat, Miss. There exist but *seven* personality cha'acter types, and they are each to be reca'nized according to which of the so-called seven deadly sins—or nasty disposi- tions—predominates. We can't help any of it, so no fret- tin' over hot weather, sour milk, or moon trouble. You, for example, are held fast in the chill grip of Vanity . . .") Outside the window, Central Park lay awakened in the present, in springtime.

"You're ready for wardrobe now, Miss Wayfaring."

What shall we eat, what shall we drink, what shall we put on our broad back?

She had written that same afternoon, "I have become enormous," and had begun to become obsessive about the look of it written down, like someone feigning interest in the time, looking at a new watch over and over again.

We shall eat, drink, and put on more of the same.

"I suppose I'll have to wear that *schmatta* Omar the tentmaker ran up for me yesterday—or else sit here and *schvitz* while they all suffer through *Avenged.*"

"That *schmatta*," Cégèste observed, "is a glorious and costly shot-silk Framboise!"

"So it is. Listen, honeybunch, I get down on my knees every night and every morning—keep my shoes under the bed so I remember. So, which shoes, the gold ones?"

"Your instinct is unerring."

"Instinct? Left to my instincts, I'd probably succumb to immortal longings."

"You're immortal already," Georgie thrust in; "you're a household word."

"Tell me this, should I wear this to match the shoes?"

She picked up what looked to them like a gold-link necklace, and held it up like a string of pearls, or a strip of film, reading it from behind. Cégèste and Georgie read from the front as she held it across her neck, the legend EVERYTHING'S TRUE.

"Got it from another household word, my esteemed director, the old buzzard. He heard it in California, of course."

"Everything's true that's useful," Georgie declared, putting away the implements of his art.

"Georgie, you have evidently been around the block a few times."

"Wear it," Georgie advised, "but don't wear it out if you're walking alone. They're ripping it off your neck these days on Madison Avenue and showing up next morning on Santa Monica Boulevard selling it out of brown paper bags. That's what bi-coastal means in the eighties, Miss Wayfaring."

"The operation you've just outlined sounds exactly like what the typical Eastern Seaboard intellectual thinks motion-picture dealing is. Now tell me this," Kaye added.

"There's the screening, and then the parties. Do you think it's true or not that everything happens at parties?"

"Everything's true, isn't it?"

"My mother would have loved you."

Everything's true, but not everything is so, she advised herself severely.

Yes, yes, but how do you *feel?*

Remember the feeling cube.

In one of those hysterical extension courses at Yale C.W. sent us to.

What was his name, that poor man?

The cube had six—no, eight corners.

Good God, would you look at that creation they just brought in to throw over her.

Eight cardinal attitude points. Four pairs of opposites, as I recall. Each and every feeling one's poor self gets sent erupts at some specific affective point co-ordinate within. Self-therapeutic spelunking, he called it: the way out is the way in. I could play with that again—improvising.

Imagine a seven-pointed polyhedron, for example, enclosing every variable in the affective arsenal, the capital repertoire: let's see if I can do this that Jameson taught me out on the beach. *Invidia. Avaricia. Superbia.* It's a tango, a samba, a beguine . . . *Ira* . . . *Luxuria* . . . *Libido* . . . *Accidia.* I love that one . . . *Accidia,* my life is an *Accidia.* Somewhere in there your feeling quivers, unacknowledged and unnamed. Reach in to it; it knows it belongs to you. . . .

"Here, now, Miss, get into this."

Invariably, in entertainment crises, her mother, having fashioned at the last minute some costume or other out of disparate remnants, would march out of the sewing alcove

and direct Diana Kaye, and life would start over with yet
another entrance.

Two to get through, she thought: the one at Tavern-on-
the-Green and the other one at the Café des Artistes.

> *It was in the fresh air,*
> *And we went as we were*
> *And we stayed as we were*
> *Which was Hell . . .*

God help me, why do I think of that? Because it's
thoroughly true?

"WHAT is it she thinks she wants?"

"Perhaps a little something further in the respect and
recognition line."

"Aw, wisha—it's nineteen eighty-one here, man."

"No thanks to you."

Jameson O'Maurigan, the scripter of *Avenged,* and Orphrey Whither, its producer/director, stood together on
the outdoor balcony of the Metropolitan Opera House,
which Orphrey Whither called "the theater," looking back
and forth between the roofs of the buildings he called "the
music hall" and "the dance hall."

"You realize, don't you, that she's a divergent sensation
type, and tends towards a certain schizophrenia," the director informed his collaborator.

"Ballocks!"

"I speak the truth, which is rarely pure and never simple.
I say she tends on certain evidence. The mother was mad,
and the aunt. The brother gave himself a drowning death.
The legendary cousin behaved similarly."

"That legendary cousin," said Jameson, looking away, "was my beloved friend."

"Many a beloved's dead," said Orphrey Whither accusingly, pointing down at the plaza. "Civilization goes on. The living of a life goes on—promptly, in whatever condition. You're still expressing yourself."

"You're the most offensive man in New York."

"I'm old; I say what I like—and it's all true—while you whimper about respect."

KAYE WAYFARING stared out the window again.

I've had it with those fuckers, I swear I have.

She stubbed out a Lucky Strike and reached across an arm's-length space to press the Play button on her companionable Sony cassette machine. After a plaintive and extended orchestral introduction, the voice of Mawrdew Czgowchwz, singing Richard Strauss's *"Morgen,"* filled the room and soothed her rage.

Und morgen wird die Sonne wieder scheinen . . .

Tomorrow, yes, tomorrow, as Rock Hudson promised Jane Wyman at the end of *Magnificent Obsession*, the picture that had changed her life once and for all, in nineteen fifty-four, in Atlanta.

She paced the floor, regrouping her forces—the voice of Mawrdew Czgowchwz now declaiming *"Es gibt ein Reich"* from *Ariadne auf Naxos*.

Es gibt ein Reich wo alles rein ist:
Es hat auch einem Namen: Totenreich.

They told me to take a streetcar named "Desire" and get off at the Elysian Fields. . . .

Oh, paper boy—come here, paper boy! Has anybody ever told you you look like a prince out of the *Arabian Nights?*

> *Hier ist nichts rein!*
> *Hier kam alles zu allem!*
> *Bald aber naht ein Bote,*
> *Hermes heissen sie ihn.*
> *Mit seinem Stab*
> *Regiert er die Seelen:*
> *Wie leichte Vögel*
> *Wie welke Blätter*
> *Treibt er sie hin*
> *Du schöner, stiller Gott! sieh! Ariadne wartet!*

She stood in the doorway arch, with her hands at her sides, and let her arms reach the short distance on each side until the backs of her hands were touching the sides of the door frame, and then she made a tight fist with each hand. She pressed each fist hard against the door-frame sides until pain shot up her arms, and then, opening the fists, she dropped her arms and stepped into the room again. Her arms, lifting by themselves, seemed to carry her aloft, most certainly in spirit. "God bless that old girl at school," she said, smiling.

> *Du wirst mich befreien,*
> *Mir selber mich geben,*
> *Dies lastende Leben,*
> *Du nimmst es von mir.*

An dich werd' ich mich ganz verlieren,
Bei dir wird Ariadne sein.

The car containing Orphrey Whither had arrived and was waiting below in the inner courtyard. Miss Wayfaring sallied forth.

GONERIL DREENE sat at the long table in the press room, poring over Hyperion Productions' press release on *Avenged.*

"Made over four years, at a cost of eleven million dollars . . ."

The door slammed shut; the unit publicist and the *Variety* stringer ambled into the bright room.

"Look who's working! You're a better man than we are, G.D."

"Oh, it's you. Did you write this little dispatch, Bozo? It's a stitch."

"I did not," the publicist replied. "If there's one thing I hate worse than the pictures, it's the releases."

"You're going to the party, aren't you?"

"They're making two parties, one at the Green and another one at the Daze Arrivistes later on at midnight."

"Such panache—and you and your sidekick have been having a party rehearsal."

"Listen, it's like Gloria Gotham says, 'Everything happens at parties.' We're in the prophecy industry; prophecy is thirsty work."

"So, what about Wayfaring? Is she dancing solo, or is she bringing the new main squeeze?"

"Looks like solo," the stringer interposed, "unless the squeeze fits under the dress."

"Always a thrill to hear you. Grab you later, topside, in the dark."

THE FOUR klieg lights, positioned at the corners of the plaza like huge glass drums, were switched on at the stroke of eight, sending long shafts of blue-white arc light into the dense, layered evening sky to crisscross one another. A satellite spun overhead: a sphere reminiscent of the long-vanished logo of the original Universal Pictures, it featured a band of "revolving effect" light-bulb lettering advertising "Kaye Wayfaring in *Avenged.*"

From the roofs of Avery Fisher Hall and the New York State Theater, multiple krypton lasers projecting beams in crisscross lattice fashion off assorted oscillating mirrors affixed to the balconies of the two buildings, into a matrix of fog which rose from open barrels ringed around the base of the fountain, hatched a red, yellow, blue, and green cartoon of the head of Kaye Wayfaring as Candace, the heroine of *Avenged,* with her ophidian hair blowing in the night wind, hovering in billboard dimension forty feet over the plaza.

"Lord, what an apparition!" Mawrdew Czgowchwz exclaimed. "It captures the expression, all right."

One of Mawrdew Czgowchwz's two limousine companions, the Countess Madge O'Meaghre Gautier, turned to the other, Boadicea Tillinghast, and remarked, with emphasis, "It took the very Kaye Wayfaring to bring this woman over to the West Side and into this theater!"

"It's not the Roxy, is it?" Mawrdew Czgowchwz observed with equanimity.

"The things we're living to see! The stage door, please."

The limousine continued north up Broadway and then turned left down Sixty-fifth Street, its turn intersecting the arc of an identical vehicle turning left into the approach lane to the plaza.

"Look at them," Kaye Wayfaring said to Orphrey Whither, looking out the back window. "Why can't we go down that same way?"

"We've made the turn."

"Can't we turn back? You're the director of the picture."

"If this car pulls up at the plaza and you don't get out of it . . ."

"I should have gone with them in the first place."

"This is the part you used to think was funny."

"Vot vuz, vuz."

"In any event, there's something I want you to see."

"So I hear. Funny, you wouldn't let me look at it even last week. I understand why I have to be here tonight—I'm to affirm 'bankable'—but you needn't pretend—"

"It's that I want you to see," Whither said, pointing up. "What— Oh, my God!"

Quicker than her reaction, Kaye Wayfaring felt herself pulled from the limousine and set on course as firmly and mechanically, she remembered, looking back, as a Panaflex camera on a track.

She'd hated doing this for as many years as she'd been cajoled and bulldozed into it. Once, in Clayton, she'd been carrying a tray of cocktails from the kitchen out into the back yard, attempting an entrance, and had tripped over a distraction, becoming egregious for a long enough instant to recall later while earnestly compiling a list of grudges. ("She ain't nevuh goin' be no akaholic, Buck—she got no damn respect fer the stuff!") At the time of this summing up of grudges, in New Haven, the acting students had been given a "coming into a room" exercise, and Kaye had enraptured the small assembly of classmates in the main theater by doing her most winning, airy, *distrait* lady entrance—copied from Katharine Cornell—and capping it with a headlong pratfall she'd mastered in competition with her brother. (Jackson had broken his nose and had thereby been turned by the gods' intervention into an even more devastating boy—where was the justice in life?—but he was long dead, and no contest would ever command her interest again; no distraction comfort her. She wouldn't fall down for them.)

She put her dark glasses on.

"They know who you are, you know."

"Very funny—you ought to be in pictures."

"No autographs this evening?"

"Cousin, I am never signing anything again."

IN THE half-dimmed auditorium, Kaye Wayfaring removed her dark glasses and put on her regular ones.

Might as well see who the hell's here, after all. Oh, her. Hello, dearie, loved your book. Oh, hello there, loved yours, too. No, sweetie, I haven't; I'm saving myself. Another picture? I might. Look at you all! Did the management give all you folks reaction cards?

The lights went out; the music swelled; the credits rolled. HYPERION PRODUCTIONS PRESENTS: KAYE WAYFARING IN *AVENGED:* A FILM BY ORPHREY WHITHER. COLOR BY TECHNICOLOR . . . Kaye Wayfaring sat back and watched.

Candace slapped her lover in the face. He seized her

wrist and twisted it. "You're hurting me," she cried, pulling back, astonished. The camera, tracking in a one-hundred-and-thirty-degree arc, revealed Candace's riverfront atelier, a loft room full of statues of goddesses: Kwan-Yin, Kali, Artemis, Isis.

"We have to stop hurting one another."

"Why? It's an honest living."

"I can't do it any more."

"All right, we'll stop. I'll stop first—I call that fair."

"We can't stop. I've got to find somebody I don't have to hurt to feel alive."

"You're not alive—you know that."

Nobody's laughing; they're entrapped, Kaye Wayfaring remarked in silent wonder. Out the window on the screen, the sky over Hoboken blazed in magenta streaked with cobalt, orchid, and lime.

"Look at that sky—it's a matte!" a voice whispered from somewhere behind.

"Orphrey gives definitive sky; it's his mark."

Amazing how much I want to smoke, watching myself smoking. You can't smoke in this temple.

The plane took off from New York bound for Los Angeles. Lap dissolve . . . establishment: the Hollywood hills: the house on Elusive Drive. Kaye Wayfaring told herself: Here it comes. Orphrey had said, "I don't want you coming along. We'll shoot everything and bring it back; it's all long shots. The point is, no matter where she ends up being, she never *goes* anywhere; she's never *been* anywhere. I can't risk having your reticular intelligence soaking anything up, so stay put, and don't brood, there's a dote, it's trashy to brood."

Sooner or later I've got to go back out. For the goddam

ceremony. Probably even sooner to get seen on the town. They've got to give it to me this time.

Acrylic sky. Flamingo dusk. Shadows in Bronson Canyon. Rendezvous in Silver Lake. The double at the wheel of the white Porsche winding up Mulholland Drive. Busy acting dangerous.

Moving right along . . . I've got the Academy Award. What next?

"Are you crazy? She's absolutely breathtaking! Anyway, shut *up*, she's right over there."

Do you love it? She thinks they're home in bed in Larchmont, looking at a Betamax.

Candace and the ingenue and the ingenue's mother waiting together in the wings of the Metropolitan Opera House for the ingenue's entrance as the spirit of Aura in the adagio sequence *"Auprès de la Cascade"* from the ballet *Les Dames de Bois de Boulogne.* On the soundtrack the voice of Mawrdew Czgowchwz singing Berlioz' setting of Théophile Gautier's *"La Spectre de la Rose."*

"Caddie, I can never thank you. You've brought my baby back to life."

"Nonsense, Alta, I'm merely the privileged instrument."

Ye gods and little fishes, they're swallowing it whole. I must admit it looks fabulous. If that's me, I've never seen myself. The mother is my mother . . . I'll rot in hell.

In the fourth row of the orchestra the critic Philander Dreene passed a note, written in phosphorescent ink, to his sister Goneril. "She is walking the tightrope to greatness. There has been nothing like it since Jeanne Eagels in *The Letter!*"

Goneril glanced down, read quickly, and, looking back up agape in high awe, resumed her long-awaited love affair with Kaye Wayfaring in *Avenged.*

. . .

THE PROTAGONIST had failed; the hero and the ingenue had fought and won. Candace was pictured dead four ways in succession, none of them conclusive, all visions, expressions of her autoerotic self-loathing. She would not die. "I am she who lives through it all" was her terrifying device.

Kaye overheard a conference of whispering viewers.

"I don't get it—where is she?"

"She's in the bins."

"No, she is not in the bins—she's in a nunnery."

"She's in a what?"

"A nunnery—a *con*vent."

"That can't be done."

"You're looking at it right now."

"I don't believe it for a minute—it's too damn operatic."

"Look at that sky!"

Orphrey told her to stand up. An enormous audience, also standing, roared up at her.

He did it, the old warthog. Let me get to look that way —I wouldn't know that woman from Adam's off ox. I wanted him dead on a slab—and so what now. I owe it all to my director.

At the Tavern-on-the-Green, members of the privileged first-night audience of *Avenged* were paying tribute to its star, to stardom, to comeuppance, and to the past.

"She'd have been fifty-five. I can't picture it, can you?"

"No. What's Wayfaring, forty?"

"She was thirty-six: the last number on the roulette wheel. No, Wayfaring's still thirty-nine. Look at her waving that cigarette."

"There is that about her which is very definitely Republic Pictures."

KAYE pulled Jameson aside, into a recess in the topiary hedgerow. "My direction is exit."

"They've categorically lost their minds over you. The pale has been gone beyond."

"You remember we talked about Racine?"

"I have never forgotten."

"Help me now, then."

"I live for you from this out," the poet declared.

"Meet me at the garbage pails."

"The garbage pails?"

"In exactly four minutes."

"If I get there first, I'll write 'Go' on the wall. If you get there first, rub it out."

"There'll be a carriage waiting," Kaye Wayfaring enjoined. "Engage him."

"You realize, of course, we'll never make it to the frontier."

"We're not bound for the frontier."

"The suspense is terrible."

"I'll make it last, I promise."

"I'm yours: these are Irish hands."

Smiling, waving, never looking sideways, she followed a busboy into the kitchen and, once inside, swept past the idling cooks and the porters preparing salads, down the spiral staircase into the cellar, and at the end of four minutes had come up the outside cellar stairs and was standing in the shadow cast by a cross-park-road light on an ailanthus in the courtyard, into which a hansom cab had driven, as prearranged.

Jameson slipped over the low wall and through the sparse underbrush. Below him in the cross-drive, motor traffic sped west to east. He approached Kaye Wayfaring.

"Diana of the Crossways."

"Come on, genius, let's make tracks."

"Where to, the El Dorado?"

"We're going to the Rock of Ages, hard by the Tunnel of Love."

The driver had been told the way. They drove north on the bridle path, parallel to the barrier wall bordering Central Park West, so that the sound of the horses' hooves, thudding on turf rather than clapping on the concrete roadway, seemed to tell them they were riding in a rural situation, far away from limousines, neon display, flashbulbs, and suppers, yet they reminded one another that each of their names was scrawled on a place card at the Café des Artistes, whereto, even as they spoke, numbers of the compulsive were bent upon repairing, as they put it, haste-post-haste, for midnight delicatessen and extended carousing.

"I am not the bread of life," the star growled. "Let 'em eat taramasalata and blancmange."

"You're perking up," the poet declared. "Did you possibly like what you saw up there on the screen tonight?"

"One did not flee the theater. Tell me the truth: is it any good, or is it just a very big camp?"

" 'What is truth?' asked Pilate, washing his hands, before plunging them into the blancmange to retrieve his dropped monocle."

"You shouldn't be talking like that. Tomorrow is Easter Sunday."

"I'll wake up pure; so will you: redeemed by Mawrdew Czgowchwz, who thinks you are the best there is."

" 'Tomorrow, yes, tomorrow,' like in *Magnificent Obsession.*"

" '*Und morgen wird die Sonne wieder scheinen.*' "

"I don't think I'll wake up at all. I think I'll stay up, for a change, reading something sensational in the train."

"If it's still there in the wall."

"Where would it go?"

"Into legend; into myth."

"No, the letter is in the tunnel wall, and my mother's diary is in the bank vault in Clayton. Reality's like that."

The cab drove north through the gully, passing below street level the Majestic and the Dakota, then turned east in the direction of the Ramble.

FROM the top of the rock overlooking the Gill, they looked down at the boat lake.

"Four years of my life. Four years!" Kaye Wayfaring exclaimed.

"Indeed, and look at you now."

"What does *that* mean, in the dark?"

"Only, for example, that four years ago in the spring when we started, you couldn't make your way up here on foot, svelte as you looked, and they built the stairs next to the scaffolding for the Panaflex. That we started without steady-cam, and switched: a metaphor, if you like. And all that fall, the first year, you sat and smoked on this rock, and read publicity, as if publicity were anything to read, and talked a lot about Ariadne on Naxos, and what an ersatz Bacchus poor old Whither Pudding made when he stormed up here day after day: when would you answer to his toot. That season upon season, sixteen, count 'em, sixteen, you advanced, evolved, retrenched, and advanced again, and that I for one do love you and am proud of you. That's about it."

She held his arm. "I'm glad I asked. I love you, too; you're the best."

"Only a pale reflection. Come on, then, let's check the safe—it is why we came."

They crossed over the top of the hillock and took the stone steps down to the steep-vaulted narrow tunnel that leads from the inner Ramble to the shore of the boat-lake inlet, entering it at the east end. Kaye snapped open the small handbag with handles on it. She removed a flat mallet and a slant-edged chisel and handed them singly to her accomplice. The light from the Park lamp standing at the tunnel's entrance shone on just that section of the inner wall they meant to work on.

"Why should I imagine it isn't still there?"

"Like you said before, four years. The scene we shot right here in the tunnel ended up on the cutting-room floor. Perhaps you think the events of that afternoon never took place a-tall."

"Really, you encourage me!"

"To be consistent, always."

"I'll hold," she offered. "You chop."

"I'll hold, I'll chop. You look out."

"There's a pistol in my purse."

"I know—spare me."

"Know what I miss?" Kaye Wayfaring declared, looking up at the moon. "Black-and-white."

"I know—the highlight on the barrel."

"Exactly. *Deception.* Bang."

"Your perfume makes me crazy," said Jameson, placing the chisel. "What is it?"

"*Film Noir.*"

79

"Well, stand upwind and hum something. I'll never finish this if you distract me with fragrance. Anyway, you're in my light."

Kaye saw the light of late October, gleaming as it chilled the town. She saw herself years younger, sitting on the flat rock, looking up at the trees, and thinking about what Nazimova had written. "I am the Aeolian harp hung high in a tree for the wind to blow upon." Kaye thought herself more Miss Otis, regretting, or that other trollop, the Lorelei. Certainly not the White Rock girl.

She watched her boon companion chipping away at the tunnel wall.

And so, she thought, as Thalia Bridgewood had said one long night since in Milledgeville, there's always somebody to make the stone flat for you to stand on. (Olmsted, Vaux, somebody.) She remembered that autumn, the first of four spent shooting *Avenged*. She'd aged, she felt: *un coup de vieille*. It had been the worst of times—and then one day the Mawrdew Czgowchwz letter, and Jacob Beltane the younger.

She had read it through and come to a quick decision. Like certain passages in literature, or from two or three of her pictures, and like one or two each of her mother's convincing strictures and apostrophes, she had learned it word for word. Over the years, she had lost most of it. It was time to dig it out and read it again, on the train.

"What?" she asked, responding to Jameson's intrusion.

"I said, I can't say I'd blame them either."

"Who?"

"Why, the highwaymen on the road into the capital, of course."

"No, come on, who?"

"*Tiens, tu viens d'avoir un rêve éveillé.* You're sure you want to come back? You look grand on the moon."

"The men are disappointing—worse than the ones on Naxos. Who's not to blame—what not for?"

"The underground narcs who patrol the Park in drag, if they clapped us in irons and hauled us down to Centre Street."

"I would offer them my shoes."

"You came back to life at a crucial— Ah, here it is, and in perfect condition!"

Jameson held up the Lucite container in which Mawrdew Czgowchwz's letter had been folded and deposited over four years before, and stuck the brick back into the tunnel wall with aplomb.

"Give it to me!" Kaye cried impatiently.

"Come again, Your Majesty?"

She reared her head and laughed. "Just remember: you may be the high priest, but I'm the high priestess!"

"You're enchanting in moonlight. Furthermore, the cab is waiting to take us back."

"I'll read the letter on the train. By then it will be tomorrow."

AT THE Café des Artistes they were a hundred and one to dinner.

"Miz Dreene, what are you writing?"

"A note to myself about that picture."

"*Avenged,* an allegory of—"

"Allegory, my foot! It's *Back Street,* finally done the right way."

Neither O'Maurigan nor Wayfaring had yet arrived.

81

Orphrey Whither and some gadabouts were cluttering up the bar, halfheartedly discussing dispatching a posse.

"I saw them head off that way. . . ."

"I call it rude."

"Western Civilization is not, in New York, run on manners, Miss Dreene. They drew you a fake bill of goods on that one, altogether, I'm sorry to have to tell you."

"I call it rude all the same."

Mawrdew Czgowchwz and the Countess Madge O'Meaghre Gautier sat apart with Patrick More, the leading man in the picture, and Boadicea Tillinghast.

"She was just sensational. You were too, Patrick More, simply sensational."

"Thank you, Mrs. Tillinghast."

"My mind is running backward," Mawrdew Czgowchwz declared. "I see her hovering forty feet over Lincoln Center."

"Where *is* she, that hooligan?" The Countess Madge O'Meaghre Gautier scowled.

"If I were she, I'd be home changing into a little black dress," Mawrdew Czgowchwz offered.

"What becomes of most legends? They change into little black dresses. We are observed. Look at that poor Dreene personage. Creature! She looks hungrier than Dolores ever did!"

"Those were the days, dear," said Boadicea Tillinghast. "Something sensational to read every morning. No more."

"That part of those days was appalling," said Mawrdew Czgowchwz, drawing her stole about her. "One hated it then, and one hates the memory of it now."

"Ah, yes," crooned the Countess Madge. "True stars needed never campaign in those days. When Mawrdew

Czgowchwz won the Academy Award for *Pilgrim Soul* a generation ago, she got it straight from God. It came *sailin'*, like, right through the picture window, never even breakin' the pane!"

"You doubt my sincerity?" the diva remonstrated.

"Would you like an Academy Award, Patrick?" the Irishwoman cooed. "You must ask Madame Czgowchwz how to get one. Madame Czgowchwz knows all about it."

"That I do not," Mawrdew Czgowchwz countered, "but we were discussing Miss Wayfaring and her performance."

"There are, I believe, certain marked parallels."

MEANWHILE, Orphrey Whither had cornered a M. Thérion, the film correspondent of the French intellectual journal *Quoique*.

"*Un cinémetteur peut tourner les films les plus exquis du monde, mais s'ils sont projetés devant des salles vides, il est bloqué; il n'a rien obtenu ni pour l'art ni pour l'humanité. Pour distraire le spectateur moyen, il vous faut une histoire intime—et une histoire exige de bonnes scènes à deux personnages—parfois d'avantage, mais fondamentalement deux personnages. Par example, Mademoiselle Wayfaring et Monsieur O'Maurigan—la déesse américaine et le poète irlandais . . . qu'est-ce qui s'est passé depuis leur. . .*"

JAMESON stood talking to the hansom-cab driver at the small gold-painted Ruritanian guardhouse in front of the Dakota.

"I seen huh on the news heeh. She got big, man, but she's still terrific-lookin'!"

"She is very beautiful."

"You know huh as a person?"

"We've been close friends for some years."

"You kinda look after huh, right?"

"I think she's rather good at doing that for herself."

"What I mean is, you know, she's inna public eye—they got lunatics out dere."

"I think I know what you mean."

"I dink she's great. I don't wanna read about huh like *that* inna paper onna subway onna way t'work. My right?"

"You're right."

"Needa do you. . . . Heeh she comes."

"*Qu'est-ce qui s'est passé*— Ah, here come the companion devils!"

"Mr. Whither," Kaye Wayfaring, approaching, drawled. "What drivel have you been pouring into this adorable person's ears. *Bon soir*, Jean-Loup, *ça va?*"

"Miss Wayfaring is after feeling her Cheerios!" Orphrey Whither remarked.

"I could eat a horse on toast!" she broke out, crossing down into the dining room.

Mawrdew Czgowchwz rose to greet her. "Here you are —what a remarkable dress!"

"We've been on a treasure hunt, the bard and I—to the tunnel below the rock."

"Find anything?"

"Yes, something sensational: your letter of that October four years ago."

At the time of her receipt of the letter, Kaye Wayfaring's acquaintance of Mawrdew Czgowchwz had not been intimate. The diva's life, crowded with incident and freighted with sorrow, had not called her into it to any office other than that of admirer, until, she remembered, having gone up to Manitoy to do a summer Shakespeare season, she had met two young boys, twins, whose remarkable intelligence and whose striking looks had made her remember her brother, then long dead. . . .

"They put you here next to me," Mawrdew Czgowchwz whispered.

Patrick More, excusing himself, went to the foot of the table.

"Dashing hell-rake; always was," Mawrdew Czgowchwz declared.

"I fell in love with him opposite you in *Pilgrim Soul.*"

"No less than I, I can assure you. That was a complication you have avoided this time around, working with the morsel."

"But I'm in love with your son."

"I was in love with his father. That didn't stop the libidinal music."

"This is very confusing."

"Indeed. To other topics. Your performance: perfect."

I had better simply go along and listen to everything she tells me.

"You think it works?" Kaye Wayfaring asked, with a degree of uncertainty that made her blush.

"It's perfect; no argument. No high mass about affect. You conveyed the scenes, not the moods."

" 'No men's scented pieties.' I remembered that from your letter."

"Did I mean to be a sponsor or a scold? I've badgered myself."

"All day long I've been brooding about men. They're not to be believed."

"No, they are not. Perhaps not even aroused from sweet slumber." Mawrdew Czgowchwz threw off her stole. "Could I have one of your Lucky Strikes? I haven't had one in years. I find them evocative, but of what I disremember."

"They remind me of a man, of course: of my father."

"That's generally the one."

"What do I want you to tell me, anyway?" Kaye asked.

"Probably what will happen. 'A mother knows everything.' That ancient carol."

"Mine always insisted it."

"It's perfectly true, so far as it goes. What she probably didn't tell you is that Mother doesn't look to; it's visited upon her. You'll find out soon enough."

"You see that in the cards, eh?"

"I see these men making their mirrors to look into."

SHE's withholding. What is she withholding? She's Irish. She's Bohemian. She's mystical. She's his mother. She should be mine. Here's the food. I'll worry about all this after supper.

They were served *pigeons confits aux raisins, tarte aux champignons, chicon,* and *coeurs flottants.*

"One thing I might do up there on Manitoy with him," Kaye Wayfaring said, "is put an end to my Ariadne obsession."

"I had one of those for years," said Mawrdew

Czgowchwz, looking away, "before I became Per-
sephone."

"Your life would make a sensational picture."

"Who'd be me, you?"

"It's a four-o'clock-in-the-morning Orphrey Whither
idea."

"I might just go for it one fine day, but I think *Another
Day: Tomorrow* is the more sensational scheme by far."

"I'm to take the treatment with me up to Manitoy. Orphrey says if I win the Academy Award, he'll make anything I like next. He said it in front of reporters. What is
it, 'The one hand washes the other'?"

"The better that each may wave," said Mawrdew
Czgowchwz, waving at a face across the table.

"Of course, on the other hand, I may never make another motion picture."

"What's going *on* down there?" Goneril Dreene hissed to
the *Variety* stringer.

"They're being stars together."

"Wildly inconsiderate!" observed the scourge of *Pomander Walk*.

"They forget the fact we made them what they are
tonight. They always forget that. They always have: it's
their predatory nature."

"That's a fact. They're simply a couple of media crea-
tions."

"The pen is still mightier than—whatever."

"When did *you* last see a *pen?*" the vainglorious woman
cackled. "I'd love to get a gander at your hot item tomorrow."

"I phoned it in before, without the specifics. Nowadays it's the names, not what the names are up to."

"This is the truth, the deep truth. Look, Mawrdew Czgowchwz is standing up."

"Bubbles that burst."

"Quiet, this is exciting!"

MAWRDEW CZGOWCHWZ had been asked to sing. Orphrey Whither had proposed, in what Boadicea Tillinghast later described as "an access of nostalgia," that she do a few operatic turns, assisted by friends. "My three favorite things you ever did were the Violetta, the Delilah, and the Katisha!"

Kaye Wayfaring looked closely at Mawrdew Czgowchwz with, she thought, the greatest admiration she'd ever felt for anyone, simply for putting up with that kind of talk from the old *omadhaun*.

"There's nothing like a little vaudeville after the picture, is there?" the ultimate diva remarked, by way of acquiescing.

PHILANDER DREENE, on a quick hop across town, having left the Checker cab, motor running, below, entered a penthouse foyer on East Seventy-ninth Street as the party following a poetry reading at Books and Company was breaking up.

"I must dash *right* back over—they're preparing musical charades!"

"Mr. Dreene, you should be a little less relentless with yourself," one of the two hosts responded, in the cordial and faintly alarmed voice of south central Georgia.

"Hushed be this said," the itinerant replied, "but I feel I must be on to everything."

"A large audience of the most serious listeners in the city is most grateful to you."

"I must confess I do rather consider *Midnight Oil* a fertile oasis in the airwaves wasteland. And tonight I've got Halcyon Paranoy, on location, so to speak, dining with Mawrdew Czgowchwz, Kaye Wayfaring, Orphrey Whither—and now I've got *you*. New York, New York!"

"Here's our tape," the second host, a Philadelphian, offered. "Hope they like it. And please give our very best to Miss Wayfaring."

"They'll like it all right, the lot of 'em. This is a great night in town. Every diehard scene-maker— I must dash. I hope to get a turn or two recorded."

Philander Dreene wriggled into the crowded elevator just as the doors were closing.

"Don't let me step on anybody's— *Hello!* I've just come from the *Avenged* premiere. She gives . . ."

RE-ENTERING the apartment, the second host inquired of the first, "Are we getting on that train?"

"We've got hours. Time enough to play through the entire Covent Garden *Fanciulla*—O'Maurigan's consolation offering for cutting us off his dance card on this stellar New York night."

"Mawrdew Czgowchwz in her favorite role and in her prime. It was wonderful seeing her name again this afternoon in Gloria Gotham. 'Mawrdew Czgowchwz, slated to attend the *Avenged* fete . . .'"

"Ah, yes, Gloria Gotham, the diehard scene-makers' racing form. What would life be without benevolent dictation?"

"Pity we couldn't be with the Wayf in her triumphant hour. I was telling a fan of yours earlier about that Yaley Daily review of her Millamant. 'Mark these prophetic words . . .'"

"One likes to think one helped in some small way."

"I'm sure you do—I mean did," the Georgian said, smiling. "Why don't you call her over there—now?"

"Call the *West Side?* Listen to this: it's the poker game!"

The voice of Mawrdew Czgowchwz filled the room, singing the finale to Act Two of *La Fanciulla del West*— recorded at Covent Garden in the spring of nineteen fifty-seven.

> *Tre assi e un paio!*
> *E mio! Ah, è mio!*

"Listen to that!"

"Do keep an eye on the time."

"*That* is time—time out of mind!"

> *E mio . . . E mio!*
> *Ah! Ah! Mio!*

ACCOMPANIED by Orphrey Whither, Mawrdew Czgowchwz, standing in the bay of the Steinway grand, sang.

> *Tra voi saprò dividere*
> *Il tempo mio giocondo;*
> *Tutto è follia nel mondo*
> *Ciò che non è piacer . . .*

Jameson had sung the first stanza of the *"Libiamo"* in his parlor tenor-baritone, appending to the voice a dulcet head-tone extension, "sounding like a Whippenpoof," according to the Countess Madge, whom Kaye overheard whispering to Boadicea Tillinghast.

Now the two were singing alternately, in question and answer.

> *La vita è nel trepudio*
> *Quando no s'ami ancora*
> *Nol dite a chi l'ignora*
> *E il mio destin così . . .*

and then together, as many at the tables sang along,

> *Godiamo la tazza e il cantico*
> *La notte abbella e il riso;*
> *In questo paradiso*
> *Ne scopra il nuovo dì . . .*

Eyewash, all of it, Kaye thought. Yet how grand to have believed in any of it even for an evening—moreover, to have been in that business of putting it over, where you could take your work along to supper parties —not leaving the pith of you in a round tin can, prey to atmospheric conditions no lynx coat ever softened. "Look at them," she mumbled—"they look a quarter of a century younger apiece." So real was the effect Mawrdew Czgowchwz was having upon Kaye Wayfaring that the guest of honor told herself that at any moment the oltrano would collapse into a bagnoire fauteuil, gasping *"Oh, qual pallor,"* but there weren't any in the room. Instead, amid the applause, Orphrey Whither got up from the piano, and Jameson O'Maurigan sat down, as the vaudeville continued.

The Countess Madge O'Meaghre Gautier leaned sideways, whispering to Kaye, "I haven't heard the great creature so forward in these however many years. The effect you have upon her is positively evang*el*ical."

"I'm absolutely in awe, even in love," Kaye Wayfaring confided.

"That can't be helped in situ Czgowchwz," the Irishwoman avowed. "God help us to our rest."

"And me to Manitoy on that express."

"Sit tight: it won't be long more."

"But that's just it—I don't want this to end!" the star cried.

"That's the dilemma, all right."

JAMESON, at the piano, was executing the downward rondels Saint-Saëns had written to heat up the desert night in Gaza. Mawrdew Czgowchwz, her hair loosed and tumbling (become over the years a darker mineral-like titian), stood facing away from Orphrey Whither, looking over the diners' heads to the exit door, which to Kaye seemed like a pair of french windows flung open on a sultry night. The supper room was redolent of *Arpège*, *Film Noir*, *Je reviens* and *Chamade*, among other scents, and Kaye saw in her mind the pagoda tree and the magnolia's white blossoms, and the silver ash and the catalpa.

Se pourrait-il que sur son coeur
L'amour eût perdu sa puissance?

> *La nuit est sombre et sans lueur . . .*
> *Hélas! Il ne vient pas!*

He'll come all right, down to the dock: his youth and beauty and goodness on display. . . .

Goodness has nothin' t'do with it, Dearie. . . .

Not long more . . .

The way out is the way in. . . .

Orphrey Whither, sounding like a carnival barker, lunged into his impersonation of Samson.

> *En ces lieux malgré moi,*
> *M'ont ramené mes pas . . .*
> *Je voudrais fuir, hélas! et ne puis pas!*
> *Je maudis mon amour . . . et pourtant j'aime encore . . .*
> *Fuyons—fuyons ces lieux que ma faiblesse adore!*

The old fool: I'd like to tie him to a tree—or, better yet, to the crank wheel of a children's carousel.

Mawrdew Czgowchwz turned quickly, raising an arm.

> *C'est toi! c'est toi,*
> *Mon bien-aimé . . .*

The whole of *Avenged* came rushing back into Kaye Wayfaring's mind, shot for shot, with music.

This is an example of sensory overload.

Mawrdew Czgowchwz singing: her voice drifting through open french windows.

It's the wine with the dinner.

> *Mon coeur s'ouvre à ta voix*
> *Comme s'ouvrent les fleurs*
> *Aux baisers de l'aurore . . .*

93

Tomorrow, yes, tomorrow.

She was the best; she still is, Kaye Wayfaring affirmed. She is the harp in the tree, not I. I am one of the ladies of the chorus.

Whereupon the room seemed to become a kind of golden grove, and Kaye, in her mind's unfolding theater, one of the unclothed and bewildered women depicted on the café's walls, all now, with Kaye, rounded off like holograms, unbound and floating free: spectral flower-maiden Gibson girls doing the back-up for Mawrdew Czgowchwz's Delilah.

People had come in from the street to stand in the lobby of the Hotel des Artistes, adjoining the café, and tenants of the apartments above had drifted down, in varying degrees of homely *négligé*.

"We were sitting upstairs, playing her *Esclarmonde.* This is simply un-*re*-al!"

> *Dalila, Dalila,*
> *Je t'aime!"*

The ovation filled the café, spilling into the lobby and into Sixty-fifth Street.

"Theater! Theater!" Kaye exclaimed. Just like the parties back home on Warwoman Road.

Mawrdew Czgowchwz called out into the lobby. "Would anyone happen to have a kimono in his closet?"

"I do—upstairs!"

"Could I have the loan of it for this next turn?"

"I'll bring it down!"

. . .

EVERYTHING happens at parties, and all madcap families are madcap in exactly the same way, Kaye told herself directly. In Clayton, in the forties, her mother had sent her up to the attic to fetch the Stars-and-Bars in exactly this same way, only the song was "Can't Help Lovin' Dat Man of Mine." She had sat on top of the upright Bechstein and sung, draped in the oddment of bunting, "Let me lay on my back in a forty-dollar hack," and Kaye had thought then and for a very long time afterward that the lyric went "in a forty-dollar hat," until she was corrected one night at a party on lower Seventh Avenue by a Showbiz authority, an old slag-fadge who'd bawled, "No-no-no-no-*no-no-no!* 'Hack,' you darling little dress-extra. 'Hack,' as in *taxi!*"

We were a madcap family, she protested, if otherwise unfortunate.

MAWRDEW CZGOWCHWZ, in a borrowed kimono, had commenced her final number.

> *Alone, and yet alive! Oh, sepulchre!*
> *My soul is still my body's prisoner!*
> *Remote the peace that Death alone can give—*
> *My doom, to wait! my punishment, to live!*

Laughter rippled through the room; the key signature changed. Clutching closed the kimono at the neckline, Mawrdew Czgowchwz continued in four sharps.

> *Hearts do not break! They sting and ache*
> *For old love's sake, but do not die,*

Though with each breath they long for death
As witnesseth the living I! the living I!

Everyone in the lobby had come inside to hear Mawrdew Czgowchwz singing the closing in D-flat major.

Oh, living I!
Come, tell me why,
When hope is gone,
Dost thou stay on?
Why linger here,
Where all is drear?
Oh, living I!
Come, tell me why,
When hope is gone,
Dost thou stay on?
May not a cheated maiden die?
May not a cheated maiden die?

In a pig's eye, Kaye rhymed to herself, for no reason,
except perhaps, she reminded herself, that she had just
watched herself perish on the screen, a love suicide, then
resurrect.

Mawrdew Czgowchwz was addressing the applauding
throng.

"Fourth of July before last, when my accompanist friend
O'Maurigan had his birthday, we all flew out to the country,
where at Nonsuch Stix Miss Wayfaring, sitting right there,
was lighting up Long Island's South Fork, as Viola, in
Twelfth Night. Whilst roiling at the opening-night to-do,
the Countess Madge O'Meaghre Gautier—that woman
there—came out with, 'I know what, let's do a trio for the

96

man.' Dressed in odd lengths of drapery lent us by Boadicea Tillinghast—happily with us tonight—we delivered ourselves of this quick turn, which we'll do again, next, now, to ring down the curtain on this segment of the all-night festivities, if my colleagues will most kindly oblige?"

"We'll need two more kimonos, for example!" cried the Countess Madge.

I don't remember the *words,* Kaye told herself, then told herself that didn't matter at all.

"I'll get mine!"

"And I'll get mine!"

"You're both most kind—step on it!"

Mawrdew Czgowchwz, Kaye Wayfaring, and the Countess Madge O'Meaghre Gautier withdrew to the bar to confer, while Jameson O'Maurigan played the Meditation from *Thaïs.*

"Here's mine!"

"And mine!"

The two others put on their robes, and Jameson struck up the refrain

Whereupon the women sang, nearly in unison:

> *Three little maids from school are we,*
> *Pert as a school-girl well can be,*

Filled to the brim with girlish glee,
Three little maids from school!
Everything is a source of fun.
Nobody's safe, for we care for—none!
Life is a joke that's just begun!
Three little maids from school!
Three little maids who, all unwary,
Come from a ladies' seminary,
Freed from its genius tutelary—

The women ringed around Orphrey Whither, pointing fingers at him.

Three little maids from school!

KAYE WAYFARING: *One little maid is a bride, Yum-Yum—*
MAWRDEW CZGOWCHWZ: *Two little maids in attendance come—*
THE COUNTESS MADGE: *Three little maids is the total sum.*
ALL TOGETHER: *Three little maids from school!*

KAYE WAYFARING: *From three little maids take one away.*
MAWRDEW CZGOWCHWZ: *Two little maids remain, and they—*

THE COUNTESS MADGE: *Won't have to wait very long, they say—*

ALL TOGETHER: *Three little maids from school!*
Everybody in the room began to sing.

> *Three little maids who, all unwary,*
> *Come from a ladies' seminary,*
> *Freed from its genius tutelary—*

(Everybody pointed derisively at Orphrey Whither.)

> *Three little maids from school!*

"At which saturated point," Kaye Wayfaring, gesturing, told her companions in the club car on the stalled Nite-Owl Express to Boston, "Czgowchwz and the Countess Madge pulled and pushed me toward the exit door, swept me through first, and followed. The O'Meaghre Gautier had the cab idling at the curb, and seconds later Czgowchwz and I were in the back seat, rounding Columbus Circle, doffing the kimonos like those show-girls in *Forty-second Street.* 'That's that,' she said. 'You'll send for your things.' Her letter and Jameson's treatment are back there at the des Artistes, in the handbag with handles on it, so I have nothing sensational to read in the train. . . .

"As we drove past the Criterion, they were putting up *Avenged* on the marquee, first show at noon today. They had me booked as a Miss Artemis Grey into one of those little roomettes, and I think the steward clocked me right away—just the way he said, 'Miss Grey?' I kept thinking, Where are the railway carriages of yesteryear: the way Aunt Bridgewood used to make her way transcontinental, hooked onto the backs of Cannonballs, or taking whole trains and filling them with denizens of the Rialto. I thought at least a caboose, or maybe the baggage car. She gave me this."

"A pomegranate?" one of the friends remarked, in the ironic way Philadelphians inquire after information.

"Are you properly prepared?" Kaye Wayfaring countered. "From Orphrey," she said. "All I could do was sit there and stare out at the platform and remember Penn Station the way it looked when we came up from Atlanta in forty-nine, and in that scene from *Way Station*, which was a set. I sat looking at myself right in front of my face in that mirror over the sink—that sink that you have to push back into the wall if you want to sit down on the throne—anyway, while I was worrying about things of that nature: ablutions, et cetera, and feeling exactly like Alice—that awful *Disney* Alice—the train sailed into the tunnel and up and out into Long Island City and Astoria, and I was on my way to freedom—so it says here in small print, as my mother was fond of pointing out, often. I turned off the light, and as we passed through Astoria, the skyline across the river hit the mirror in the closed door and the space opened up, and I swear, with the head in the mirror just there, I was hovering over the city—just like in *Avenged*, just like that laser cartoon you saw on television. You'd both have died: what a night! I felt maybe once we cleared Astoria—you know, we did all those retakes of the fire close-ups in Astoria, in January, by which time I was, how you say, not myself, which was just what he wanted, the old bastard."

"I think I understand the significance of the pomegranate," said the Georgian gently.

"Send it along with my things. Anyway, there it was: the reflected skyline, my severed head, and the finished product, *Avenged*. We went over the Hellgate Bridge; I'd never been over it. In my day, we left for New Haven from Grand Central. It reminded me that the Indians called Tallulah Gorge down home the gateway to the underworld—but I've told you about that."

"This is Amtrak's no-frills Washington–Boston Express."

"How you say. We always took the milk train from Grand Central. You remember. Well, off we flew into the Westchester night, and I lay back remembering 'The Mysterious Traveler' and telling myself all the old stories about those fabulous train journeys, going back to the Thalia Bridgewood Special to Chicago, Des Moines, and points west—all those points west, all the way to Hollywood, California."

"Where you belonged. You told us."

"Did I bore you to death when I was at school?"

"How dare you ask that question in a stalled train?"

"Gallant. So the train stops dead somewhere outside of Bridgeport, and here we sit trading stories."

After crossing over the Hellgate Bridge, she had fallen into a state of somnolence in which unedited dream-loops of an advanced provenance jammed the channels, from which condition she had, with the wonted determination of a serious performing artist on her night off, roused herself and made her way into the darkened club car just ahead of the sleeper.

"When we saw the two of you come down that ramp— the diva and the doxy—I said to this one, 'I want a full summation of every substance, liquid and solid, we've put into our fragile bodies since lunch.''

"I was almost sorry it was you," said the Georgian poet wistfully. "We have never had a mutual hallucination."

"We'd been sitting around playing *Fanciulla,* entirely losing our minds."

"And they had you on the news. I said to myself, This beats that two-headed chicken! If they could see her now! But of course they did see you, by satellite."

"It's been too much, the whole thing," Kaye Wayfaring declared.

" 'Let Fame, that all hunt after in their lives . . .' "

"Exactly. The dressing up; the accessorizing. This is the fourth complete realization I've had on today. Fatigue."

The Philadelphian remarked: *"Dans la vie de la plupart des femmes tout même le plus grand chagrin aboutit à une question d'essayage."*

"How you say," the star snapped. *"Honi soit qui mal y pense."*

"There's distraction at every level of performance," the Georgian remarked assuredly.

"What have you two been up to in the metropolis?" Kaye Wayfaring asked.

"You haven't been opening your mail. Reading out loud from our own and one another's work."

"Life has been good to you both."

"You have to know your item."

"Is *Avenged* a masterpiece?" Addison, the Southerner, inquired.

"I haven't any idea. All I want is the Academy Award."

"Remember," asked Skip, his friend, "at school—our school—that old German I reported to you who'd brought up what Goethe had had to say about actors and their nightly loss: *Die Nachwelt flicht dem Mimen keine Kränze.*"

"That," said Kaye, "went out with high-button shoes, and with the advent of motion pictures. And it won't come back either—not like these: do you like 'em?"

She swung one foot up on the empty seat.

"Belle scarpe, da vero!"

"They're killers. Made to drop-kick several heads."

Kaye looked at them. "I should call you more often, I really should."

"Sincerity, Miss, was ever your most attractive attribute," Skip countered.

"You'll burn in hell—we all will. Severed heads! Somebody just walked over my grave."

Her two old pals merrily attacked her together.

"You might have lived another life entirely."

"Never making the papers. Getting no attention."

"You go too far," she snapped back.

"Let's have a look at that palm," dark-haired, bearded Skip demanded. "It's been a while."

"Oh, dear, I don't know that I—"

"Come, give it here. The unexamined life is not worth living, and are we not the grave of secrets?"

"I remember you once said—when I was a fledgling actress—that extracting the future from my palm was like pulling thorns out of a lion cub's paw."

"Let's see," Skip murmured, looking into Kaye Wayfaring's palm. "Where do you come from? What do you want? Where are you going? When did you last wash a dish?"

"As I recall," Addison said, "he read both your palm and your leaves."

"And he turned my case over to the board, and the board told all those things, and I asked was it the truth, and it said, 'I don't know if it's the truth, but it's the noise.' Those were the days! We lived it up—we caroled."

"I remember," Addison continued, "when you opened at the Belasco as Cordelia, in Whither's *Lear* revival. 'There it is: your name in lights,' I said. 'What you've always wanted.' You looked up and said, 'And now I want something else. Now I want it to stay there!'"

"I was showing my true colors: mean red, sheet white, and yonder blue. Tell me about *essayage,* Sonny Boy!"

"'In the midst of heat and fury and gathering adversity, do not our young lives remain an unforgettable waltz?'"

"I see something in here," Skip murmured, "that I don't think I've seen before. Has this hand recently been stung or bitten?"

"Don't answer that," Addison warned the star. "It's nobody's business."

"I was just thinking," she replied. "Those lines ought to be railroad tracks."

"I don't much care for this wayward cross on the Mount of Uranus."

"Wayward, indeed. I tell you, new lines keep appearing in this palm the way the San Andreas fault keeps redesigning southern California."

"It's always advisable to keep one's palm up to date," said Addison, "to have something sensational to read in the train."

"Just watch your tone. The fabulous have feelings. If you cut us, do we not bleed?"

When was this done to me first? she asked herself. In the

late summer of nineteen forty-five, in Milledgeville. The war was about to end. Thalia painted my face and read my palm, and said I had a future. "That is distinctly a matter of opinion," my mother said. Next in the summer of nineteen forty-eight, on the train in Wyoming, barnstorming with that senator. She read his palm, then she read mine. "You're a shoo-in, you old coot," she said to him. To me: "You have distinct possibilities: dream on. . . ."

"Whatever you're thinking," Skip said, "it's clouding the reception by making you perspire."

"I'm thinking about another train trip."

"One to California, right?"

"Seventy-one sixty-seven Sunset Boulevard, at Formosa. *La Cienega* means the swamp. Waverly Road, at Wayfaring. Silver Lake. Camarillo. Norma Jean: love goddess."

"You must tell that whole story again to clarify the reading. In any case, it's my classic perennial favorite Wayfaring saga element."

"I met her on New Year's Eve, in a flamingo-pink sunset, walking along Sunset toward a bungalow on Martel and Romaine. It was eighty-eight degrees. She knew my folks. She started calling me up. 'Hello, Wyoming, it's me —you want to go to the beach?' On the way home from Santa Monica to Twenty-nine seventeen Waverly, at Wayfaring, we'd take a secret detour and walk along Hyperion Avenue. 'Don't you just *love* Silver Lake?' she'd whisper. 'It's so mysterious!' We took the red cars out to Burbank and the Valley. 'Let's go look at the Hollywood Freeway,' she'd say, getting excited, 'it's so *sexy!*' "

"Sometimes you are so like her. They never point that out."

"Dead nineteen years this August, and as for the red cars . . ."

"Your crowd were Angelenos."

Kaye nodded, tossing her hair sideways with her left hand. "Wayfarings, Sepulvedas, Dohenys—Daddy married an Alabama Bridgewood, came East, and got respectable."

"And you got to ride on trains."

"You have heard *all* this before."

"Never on a train stuck forever outside Bridgeport, and you tell it so truly each time."

She reached across and plucked his beard. "You're too kind, as usual. Nevertheless . . ."

"Perhaps you'd like to put it on tape? We carry blanks."

"May I keep it when I'm through?"

"Of course you may. One's salary may be inadequate, but really!"

"That would be sensational. Where I'm going, it might come in very handy."

"The Mysterious Traveler."

"It's no mystery. I'm going to Manitoy, staying there until the weather gets warm, and then I'm going back into the fish state. I get off at Route One twenty-eight."

"There's a lovely beginning," Skip said, inserting a cassette and pressing the Record button. "Carry on and remember, nothing you say will be held in evidence against you."

She looked deep into the onyx window. She heard her voice telling her old friends the same story she had told them years before: the who, the what, the when, the where, the why, the how, the rest. This time they were taping it for her to take away. . . .

How in the summer of nineteen forty-eight, Theodora (Thalia), her mother's elder sister, fabled toast of the New York Rialto, had decided she (Diana Kaye Wayfaring) ought to be broken in on the boards playing Moth, one of Banquo's hapless sons, and the bearer of the asp basket in her (Thalia Bridgewood's) Shakespeare-Ibsen-Chekhov-cum-barnstorming-for-Harry-Truman tour of the Far West. How in Laramie, at the Hotel Tomahawk, Diana Kaye had taken the stage name Wyoming Wayfaring, and had worn it for a year in California. ("My ancestors, who settled Yorba Linda and Glendale, were called Persever-ance and Frequency Wayfaring.") How she and her starlet friend ("I'm old enough to be your mother. What lipstick do you feature best?") would park the Wayfaring family Nash inside Bronson Gate (Paramount Studios) and go up into Bronson Canyon to play cave women and Biblical personages, and then take off on public transportation for far-flung reaches of the exploding metropolis. How she (Diana Kaye) had been returned to Clayton, Georgia, to her mother in time for her eighth birthday, May thirtieth, nineteen forty-nine, with severe consequences. How she had become an avaricious malcontent. How she had nearly died of aggravation.

"Addy, you know what Georgia was like!" she ex-claimed, pleading her case through an act of sense-memory in exactly the same forensic manner she had mastered many years earlier as a drama student.

"Yes, dear, life at the foot of Brasstown Bald: a tad bleak, uneventful, wearing, and brutish."

"No life at all, Addy, *death!* It makes the flesh crawl right off my bones even now to think of it. It was just as terrible for you down in Valdosta. You were a genius! You still are!" She turned to Skip. "You, too."

"Luckily. But we were talking about you, or rather you were."

"Of course there were the parties that summer and for

107

many summers thereafter. That was the summer Peggy Marsh was run over by that drunken cab driver on Peachtree Street and died. She was a dear friend of Aunt Thalia's, whom she called Theodora, which was her name, but Mama always laughed anyway. I sat on the roof and cried, and I thought, That's what happens to you if you stay in Georgia, when you could go anywhere in the world with her money!"

"I'm going to cry right now."

"No, you are not, Addy, quit it. Anyway, it *is* ironic."

"What's ironic about it?" Skip demanded.

"Oh! Well, I suppose I must tell you. It's about a part in a picture. Just when I was never going to— Another terrible idea for the screen I'm addicted to."

"You mustn't speak slightingly of motion pictures, Miss," Skip advised. "Only people who can't get into them do that."

"Who's the greatest heroine in American Literature?" Kaye Wayfaring demanded, running her right hand through her hair.

"Hester Prynne."

"Oh, for God's sake! Well, who's next?"

"Scarlett O'Hara, probably, following your train of thought, but so what? You can't be doing the remake of *that!*"

"Not the remake, Grave of Secrets, the sequel."

A silence of a certain length ensued.

"Well, that is sensational!"

"That's what you saw in my palm. That must be what the cross on the Mount of Uranus means, because it's going to be uphill all the way. It's called *Another Day: Tomorrow,* and Orphrey wants it to open in Atlanta on December eleventh, nineteen eighty-nine. Are you ready?"

"A piece of revelation!" they cried in unison.

"You do love it. And this time there isn't going to be any goddam malarky about a fake *con*test! Scarlett O'Hara was my goddam great-great-grandmother Tansy Bridgewood. All the Bridgewoods know the real story; it's been preserved. It was furthermore, according to Mama, 'an attested fact that Peggy Mitchell Marsh wrote *Gone With the Wind* not only *about* the Bridgewoods, but with the absolute fixed intention that 'Thalia' should be Scarlett O'Hara on the screen, *but,* and this is documented in a letter to Jack L. *Warner* and others—that old Bette Davis was never *ever* seriously considered, except as a headstrong Yankee upstart red *herring*—Theodora would not go out to California to make a motion picture about Georgia, due to her dire and terminal loathing of the Wayfarings, whom she considered 'Papist rapists.' 'Back lot my horse's hind parts!' she told them. 'With miles and miles of good red *real* Georgia clay!' Clay! And she never did, in spite of playing Pasadena, set one foot in Hollywood, Beverly Hills, or Glendale until her death in nineteen hundred sixty-nine. So I suppose she's about to be avenged in a way by my becoming Scarlett and helping shape her fortune in the sequel."

Addison leaned forward, inquiring in a whisper, as if the recorder ought not register their conversation. "Does she get Rhett back or not?"

"She gets him—such as he is."

"Does she keep him?"

"I haven't decided yet."

Skip held her ankle and pressed. "Well, lady, you've done it—you've become a world power!"

"I just had to tell someone."

The lights went out for a moment, then came on again; the train made a noise and lurched forward.

"Now I come to think of it," Addison admitted, looking out the window, "I've probably never heard a line more gripping than 'After all, tomorrow is another day.' "

"Is that so?" his friend remarked. "Amazing the things you discover by hearing them confessed to others on trains in the night."

"You're right, Addy," Kaye agreed, "and it's going to be the first thing on the soundtrack. We'll use *her* voice—the other one they *always* had planned for that picture—in the beginning, you know, 'I'll think about it at Tara!' And then I'll be voiced in for 'After all, tomorrow is another day.' And then the crawl right to left again the way Selznick did it: *Another Day: Tomorrow.* Dynamite, no?"

"And you're going to invest seven years of your life in the role?"

"Boys, a lot is going to happen up on that screen. I'll keep busy on the stage as well."

"Do you mean to tell us that she is going to become a highly principled woman?"

"Why not? I am."

"Of that one has no question."

"I am sick of dreaming about Milledgeville and Camarillo."

Addison nodded. "It's humiliating, isn't it? We don't get over any of it by writing it down or by acting it out."

"No, we get paid. We get paid *not* to get over it—handsomely."

"Handsomely? Nobody *we* know!"

"Then you've got a better chance."

"Who's to be Rhett, Patrick More?"

"It might be good cess to put a Brit in *that* part this time. What are you writing? My forecast? A receipt?"

"No," Skip replied, "something for you to read in the train. Does Orphrey know you're en route to Manitoy?"

"As usual, Orphrey knows nothing and everything."

"I have just one more question. Who's waiting at One twenty-eight?"

"Skip!"

"Well, if I create an awkward pause, I might just get this thing written."

Kaye stood, pulling Addison up with her. "Addy and I will move across the aisle for a few minutes and reminisce about June bugs and chinaberry trees."

"And initiation rites in the Warwoman Dell!"

The train gathered momentum. The foghorn sound of the whistle addressed the night. On the Connecticut Thruway, cars seemed to slacken their speeds as the purposeful Nite-Owl Express overtook them.

"Well, Addy, what do you think: can Wayfaring re-create Scarlett O'Hara?"

"I for one have always considered you a perfect redeemer."

"Remember when we were doing that poetry in performance?"

"May fourth, nineteen sixty-five."

"I was Hero and you were Leander."

"And himself over there was Marlowe Full-charge."

"Life was a glorious cycle of song."

"A medley of extemporanea."

"And love was a thing that could never go wrong."

"And paradise on earth was Philadelphia, Pennsylvania. We were all going to go and live there."

"And make it work."

"What were we drinking that night?"

"And where is last year's shaved ice?"

"Look at the cars. You wrote a poem about the cars—about the train passing the cars. I remember: 'Indian file they run, and pirouette together'—something like that."

"Something exactly like that."

"I remember. Addy, why don't you write a play for me sometime?"

"Looking at your face in the mirror, I could promise anything."

Kaye looked at her reflected head hovering over the backsliding traffic. "The fact is I'm not my type—there you are and there it is, as the poor Brits say."

"You've had a trying night. You'll feel better about everything when you get where you're going."

" 'The only place I really want to go.' "

"Really, this is wonderful. With our faces in the window like this, and you quoting all my best lines, it's as if we were in a picture together."

"Want to be in *Another Day: Tomorrow?*"

"It might be nice to make a living wage."

"Living and partly living."

"Oh, my!"

"I know—at four o'clock in the morning, it should be Cole Porter. Remember the afternoon he died? We commiserated in the Hofbrau House singing 'Ev'ry Time We Say Goodbye.' "

112

"*New* Haven—New *Haven!*"

The friends started gathering their items together.

"Well, boys, so long."

"Why don't you call us sometime?"

"Call *me*. I plan to be in. Manitoy four-seven-seven-four."

"We'll call tonight, after the picture show."

"Hope you like it."

"This is for you," Skip said, handing Kaye what he'd written. "And here's your tape; replay it in health."

"Thanks, I can't wait."

"Give us a kiss. Think white light."

"Get off this train!"

WHITE light, my aunt. White lightnin' is more like it. Let's look at this.

ENVOY: TO KINEMATO

Exaudi nos, beata, *give us this day*
Our fade-out/fade-in, our lap dissolve.
Produce us in Technicolor: light our way
Out of the dark night's tunnel, as we of love
To you complain (Lady of moompix limelight):
Another two-faced coinage of the brain.
Envision us this day another day: tomorrow.

Mmm—how you say. Not only . . . but he's handsome enough for the screen. Let's see: she comes across this tormented Yankee carpetbagger poet in Atlanta. Decides playing him off against Rhett . . .

As the train gathered momentum and the sky out the

right windows became apparent in wavering gray values, resembling wet sidewalks, slate rooftops, and tilefish, Kaye Wayfaring commenced overhearing a new conversation, among three speakers, undergraduates. She listened.

"Is the proposition 'There's an exception to every rule' a rule or not?"

"Does the demonstrable fact that what happens always happens mean that it must have been necessarily what always was to have happened?"

She's not saying anything, Kaye told herself, smiling. She's probably decided it's unwise to arouse them from sweet slumber.

She put her foot down, stood up, and walked back toward the sleeper, past where the students were sitting.

"Everything's true, believe you me. The vortex of synchronicity is *it!*"

They looked up, flabbergasted.

"It has a certain impact, doesn't it, when said just the right way? Work hard—live and be well."

Nestled in the synchronic vortex of dreams, she found herself installed in the streamlined private car, its interior paneled in iridium and decked with round mirrors of amethyst glass. Mawrdew Czgowchwz, the Countess Madge O'Meaghre Gautier, and Boadicea Tillinghast were there, conferring with Cordelia Bridgewood Wayfaring, Thalia Bridgewood, Ruth Draper, Katharine Cornell, Miss C.W., Marilyn Monroe, and Goneril Dreene. They were all on their way to Reno to get divorced. They were all smoking Sensation cigarettes. . . .

"Prov*idence—Prov*idence next!"

She woke up remembering that she had never inhaled a Sensation.

. . .

As THE train waited in the Providence station, she stood and edged into the aisle between the rows of roomettes, looking out the window of the empty compartment opposite hers at two forlorn male undergraduates worrying over the train windows.

Perhaps not even aroused from sweet slumber . . . Although, it's Easter morning; it's tomorrow.

As the train slid forward, she entered the empty compartment and rapped hard on the window. She caught their offguard glances, held them, and blew each boy a kiss. Ecstatic, they began waving their school scarves in the morning light. She decided to seek out their companion.

She walked back into the club car and found the girl sitting, reading.

"Got a minute?"

The girl put her book down, looked up and stared. "You really *are* beautiful."

"You going into Boston?"

"Yes. They're meeting you at One twenty-eight?"

"How did you know?"

"Oh, I didn't, I only said so because *they* decided you were going into Boston and would be met by some Shamus."

"Shamus?"

"The one in Comp. Lit. decided that. He's finding the influence of Hawthorne on Raymond Chandler."

"I was crazy about Comparative Literature," Kaye said. "Everything was always happening in places like Brabant."

"Can you sit down?" the girl asked.

"Hold on to your friends," Kaye said. "Friends are what count in life. Yes, thanks."

Lowering herself into the aisle seat, she stretched her left leg across and rested her foot on the seat arm opposite.

"You like these shoes?"

I must be going crazy. I didn't mean to say that at all.

"You really are beautiful."

"I get terribly nervous."

"You mean it isn't worth it?"

"Not a whole lot it isn't."

"But your acting makes men weep."

"It gets done; sometimes I'm around. The directions are written on the package."

"My mother laughed so hard at you in *The Country Wife* that I was born the next morning."

"That was nineteen years ago come August, on Manitoy. That's where I'm going."

"I figured that—I didn't express myself."

"So, your mother . . ."

"Wait till I keep this from her."

"You needn't keep everything. You could say we met, casually, on the train, had a chat . . ."

"My mother is a serious private investigator. I'd better not bring you up."

"I know the type; so was mine."

"Is that a pomegranate?"

"Yes, it is. It's supposed to get me through the journey."

"Of course, I could always lie. I could tell her I saw you getting off at New Haven as we were getting on. That would throw her off all right."

"I'll endorse that," Kaye Wayfaring assured her.

"Of course, meeting you this way is out of the question."

"Perhaps not, considering my role as midwife to your mother. Here, take this."

"Oh, thank you. I'll give it to my mother. That'll keep her guessing."

"That's the ticket."

"You really are beautiful."

"I'm going to a house called Harking Back. You know it?"

"I went out with both the twin boys who lived there with their mother, Mawrdew Czgowchwz."

"Like 'em?"

"I liked the one with the lute. The other one was pretty remote."

"Would you have let me know this if I'd joined you earlier and told you where I was going?"

"I'd never have had the nerve."

"Now my secret's in your hands."

"I'm not especially interested in either Hawthorne or Raymond Chandler."

"How do you like the theater?"

"Love the theater."

"I'm doing *A Streetcar Named Desire* up there this summer."

"I'll be there—with my mother."

BACK in the roomette, she washed her face with oatmeal soap and rosewater, and, opening the window, let the wind in.

There's something to be said for a full-moon face: not a line on it anywhere.

She looked at the head with flowing hair, suspended in the mirror opposite.

Drop-kick severed heads indeed.

"Miss Grey? Excuse me, Miss Grey?"

"What, already?"

"Telegram, Miss Grey—got delivered at Providence."

"Slip it un— Wait a minute."

She drew back the compartment's traverse curtain. Smiling, the attendant handed her the message, tipped his cap, and withdrew.

TO MISS ARTEMIS GREY ABOARD THE NITEOWL EXPRESS

BE DOWN TO GET YOU WEARING SOMETHING FUNNY STOP

ITS ALREADY HALF PAST EIGHT STOP

YOU CANT HELP THE FACT YOURE LATE STOP

JUST BE GLAD THE BAND STOPPED PLAYING STOP

WILLOW CABIN SWEPT BEDECKED STOP

WAYS OF LIFE HERE TO INSPECT STOP

YOU ALONE SET FREE TO TELL STOP

WHAT TO DO NEXT STOP

ALL IM FOR IS HER I SEE STOP

FAR AWAY APPROACHING ME STOP

THEY WANTED MY SIGNATURE STOP

I TOLD THEM THE LADDER MAN

Dear boy. Dear destination.

There is a peaceful kingdom, a green and pleasant land, where all is . . .

The attendant walked down the hall, announcing:

"Route *One* twenty-*eight* next, Route One twenty-*eight*. Approaching Route *One* twenty-*eight!*"

He stopped on the other side of the drawn curtain and hissed in a stage whisper: "Miss Grey?"

"Yes?"

"We're coming to One twenty-eight."

"Thanks, I heard you."

"You just stay put."

"Stay put?"

"Until everybody is off."

"Do you really think that's necessary?"

"You leave it to me, Miss Grey. This is Massachusetts."

"That's exactly what they say when you cross into California."

"Well, up here we can prove it."

"I hear you."

THE GIRL looked up as Kaye Wayfaring walked back into the club car. Behind her, the attendant was occupied with passing her luggage, the single overnight case, down to a porter. In a cleared space adjacent to the Route One twenty-eight overpass, a helicopter idled. Kaye approached her confidante.

"You're going off to Manitoy in *that?*" the girl asked.

"The ferry is erratic. I recall some days it didn't run. Thank you for telling me about yourself. Look, this just came."

The girl read the telegram from Manitoy.

"If I quit school and go into the movies, will that kind of thing start to happen to me?"

"Miss Grey! Miss Grey!" the attendant called.

"Happy landing," said the girl, holding the pomegranate.

"Thanks. Listen, I've been thinking. Tell your mother the truth."

"I'll tell her I know where you are and I can't tell anybody."

"And stay in school—here, take this."

She removed the thin gold necklace and dropped it into the hand holding the pomegranate.

"I—I shouldn't accept this."

"You certainly should—it works!"

As the Nite-Owl rounded the bend beyond the overpass, the helicopter, having lifted, flew east into the sun. Borne aloft, Kaye Wayfaring resumed her career.

WINTER
MEETING

KAYE WAYFARING was handed a cordless platinum telephone. She wove through a thicket of onlookers and cut out alone across the terrace of Ralph Von Gelsen's rococo hacienda overlooking Nichols Canyon. The lights of Los Angeles were visible all the way to the Pacific. There must, she told herself, undoubtedly be an idiot-savant somewhere in there who would gladly come out here and tell me, in seconds, exactly how many of them there are.

She dialed 0–617 . . .

"Operator, this is a collect call from Artemis Grey. I'll hold, thank you."

I adore Los Angeles.

"Hello? Hello there, this is the mother of your unborn child. Listen, I've been thinking about names—androgynous names. . . . 'Jack' isn't androgynous. . . . What? Very funny. That's the last time I make certain people privy to Wayfaring family legends. He said 'If it's a girl . . .' "

I adore this troubadour.

"Who's here? Everybody's here. Bette Davis is inside, sitting where Mae West used to sit, telling stories about her."

Where are we going to live, anyway: up there on Manitoy?

"Who else? Everybody else. Do you wish you were here?"

Make me a willow cabin at your gate . . .

"We're leaving any minute for the airport. Should get to the Dakota by noon your time."

Write loyal cantons of contemnèd love, And sing them loud—

But no one is contemning.

"I know you don't: it's all right. I'll go to the show, and fly up the day after tomorrow. Meanwhile, your brother will keep me amused. He looks something like you."

As it might be, perhaps, were I a woman, I should your lordship . . .

These men. These men.

"Yes, I'll be talking to your mother. We get along famously."

Now he's feeling surrounded. Look at those lights—they're absolutely fabulous.

"Then I'll stay put; I promise."

He's not smiling.

"I'm not nominated yet. If I'm nominated, and if I win . . . we'll see."

If he threatens me, I'll tell his mother and his brother on him.

"I wish you could see these lights. Yes. If I close my eyes, I can see it, and you looking across at it."

All through the night I delight in your love . . .

"What? Yes, I suppose 'Kaye' is androgynous."

He's done it. I want to fly through the night and be there by his side.

"I've got to hang up now. People are looking this way. One last thing. I did the *I Ching* this afternoon, and threw Deliverance. I love you: let us be friends."

PLACING the phone unit on a passing butler's empty cocktail tray, the brilliant and beautiful star of *Avenged* sauntered back against a relentlessly ordered environment of plumbago, trumpet vine, hibiscus, hydrangea, catalpa, jacaranda, and coconut palm, in search of her ardent conspirator Jameson O'Maurigan. Inside, behind a sheer redoubt wall of plum Lalique glass, urgent festive activity accelerated to full tilt. Commentary ricocheted off *trompe-l'oeil* frescoed walls as livelihoods were compromised and reputations mangled.

"Are we talking 'Can we talk?' "

"Certain names have been changed to protect me from the innocent."

" 'Feel this ass—go ahead, *feel* it—hard as a *rock!*' I told her. 'Darling, you are slipping on a *wet deck!*' "

"Splashheads, the whole family."

"I went *cray*ons—cray*ola!* Corvette to Camarillo—know what I'm saying?"

"I swear to *God*, his last words were 'Cut! Cut!' I was *there*: I *heard* them!"

"They ask me, so I tell them: 'Go for the burn.' "

" 'I didn't like that guy when I was *dancin'* with him.' Everybody col*lap*sed!"

" 'Love God, and do as you will.' Isn't that *dear?*"

"Rehearsing to the *door*knob! You hear it *all* out here!"

"The only effective aging retardant is death."

Kaye spotted Jameson talking to Ralph's sister, Sequoia Von Gelsen Gay.

"Another swell party, Zeke."

"I don't know where he gets 'em. And they call *me* the queen of Hollywood casting."

"And what a night: clear as the planetarium dome. It's exhilarating!"

"Perfect flying weather. Hadn't you two better be head-ing out for Burbank? No telling how long conditions will last."

"They're fueling," Jameson said. "Whenever Miss Wayfaring is ready, we're off."

"You must be wildly happy," Sequoia Von Gelsen Gay declared, looking at Kaye Wayfaring with admiration.

"I'm never absolutely happy leaving this town."

"Look," the casting director said, "more than anybody else I *know* of in this industry, you've paid your dues. Get out of town: go have a life. You heard it here."

"Let me go touch up the face."

"Don't make me laugh, or I'll cry."

"You're too kind: you always were."

"THAT girl," said Sequoia Von Gelsen Gay to Jameson O'Maurigan, as Kaye Wayfaring walked down the corridor. "That girl—"

"She'll have her life," the writer assured the casting director. "It's been prepared."

KAYE WAYFARING studied her face in the bulb-ringed "correcting" bathroom mirror.

Leave it to him to have one of these. So this is how your echt American love goddess actually looks. I don't get it. I'm clearly not supposed to, that's all.

She turned the dimmer wheel on the wall down to Low-Key and stepped out into the corridor, turning left instead of right.

It always takes them longer to fuel up than they say it will. What's that blue light shining there? Somebody looking at black-and-white television? It's a time warp.

The room at the far end of the corridor, darkened for serious viewing, was occupied by a child whom Kaye took to be Ralph Von Gelsen's daughter Désirée.

"May I come in?"

"That depends on who you are and what you want."

Who am I? Where do I come from? What do I want? Where am I going?

"Kaye Wayfaring. Nothing much. I was just getting ready to leave."

"Come in: sit down. They never heard of doors around here."

"What's on, besides commercials?"

"*Don't Bother to Knock,* starring Marilyn Monroe. It's coming from Atlanta."

"I'm from Atlanta myself: born there. I knew Marilyn Monroe. Our birthdays were two days apart. We once celebrated them together, here in Los Angeles."

"I didn't mean to be rude. I saw *Avenged.* I cried."

"You're not rude. I know what life can be like here. I was partly raised over in Silver Lake."

"You knew Marilyn Monroe. Was she like that?" Désirée Von Gelsen asked, indicating the picture on the video screen.

"Almost exactly like that—turned way down."

They watched *Don't Bother to Knock.* The star, playing a babysitter, was talking to her charge.

"It isn't a very long story. It has a happy ending. I think that's nice, don't you?"

The little girl was looking Marilyn Monroe over.

"Are you tattooed?"

"No," Marilyn Monroe answered her, narrowing her gaze, "are you?"

"She's something else," Désirée Von Gelsen said.

"She was very beautiful," Kaye Wayfaring declared.

"She was crazy, that I know. That they told me."

"You haven't told me who you are," Kaye Wayfaring said. "Aren't you Désirée?"

"Desyrel."

"Desyrel?"

"I changed it from Désirée to Desyrel."

"I don't get it."

"I changed it from Désirée to Desyrel after the pill my father takes."

"Oh."

"He's a lot nicer on them."

They continued watching the picture without talking. Marilyn Monroe, wearing a dress and earrings belonging to the little girl's mother, had lured Richard Widmark over the hotel telephone into the room he believed was hers, and was telling him lies about leaving New York on a freighter.

"I'm going to South America tomorrow night."

"What will you do in South America?"

"I'm going to drink lots of coffee, and talk to all the parrots."

"I've got to go," Kaye Wayfaring said, hearing herself sound alarmed.

"Where to?" the girl asked. "Silver Lake? Atlanta? South America?"

"We're flying back to New York."

"Not on the red-eye: it left."

"In the Hyperion jet."

"Take me: I'm small. I won't be missed. He'll let you."

"I don't think you believe that."

"Belief is a tricky business around here."

"I'm going somewhere else from New York. I'll send a card."

"You'll be back for the Oscar? There won't be any question this time."

"You're something else yourself: you realize that."

"Do I remind you of you?"

"You remind me of the fact that I was kidnapped from Silver Lake."

"I could play it: he'd produce. He'll do anything to keep me a prisoner in this corral."

"Eat your spinach: I'll be back."

"I'll be here: at a party."

SHE REJOINED Jameson, who stood talking to an English writer who was drunk.

"She issues radiant from her dressing room / Like one prepared to scale an upper sphere / By stirring up a lower . . . ," the Briton chanted, holding his crotch, toasting Kaye Wayfaring, and spilling his cocktail all over his shirt front.

"Never leave Los Angeles, Geoffrey," Kaye Wayfaring said. "We *so* need your quality here."

"I want to say 'cunt,' but something isn't letting me."

"Oh, go ahead. Walk down that hall, turn left, and say it into the bathroom mirror. You'll feel ever so much better, I *promise* you."

She turned and led the way out of the Von Gelsen establishment.

THE HYPERION PRODUCTIONS Phaeton jet idled on the runway at Burbank airport, awaiting final takeoff clearance.

"Cigarette, Miss Wayfaring?" the cabin steward asked.

"No, thank you, Kyle."

"Anything to drink?"

"No, thank you."

"Open up the window and leave in a tiny air?" Jameson O'Maurigan offered.

"Are you driving? I hope not."

"I no longer pilot aircraft in the dead of night."

"Thank you for seeing me home."

"Partway at least. To the ferry slip on Manitoy."

"You realize, I'm happy?"

"Your happiness is lovely, and a worthwhile undertaking for all concerned."

AVIATE. Navigate. Communicate.

Shake and burble warns of stall.

Lifting, the ship leaves its shadow behind.

Even in the dead of night.

"ARE YOU asleep already?" Jameson asked.

"I was thinking about Marilyn Monroe in *Don't Bother to Knock.*"

"Imagine!"

"Signaling the dead pilot with the venetian blinds."

"I remember very well."

"Also the Von Gelsen girl."

"Désirée?"

"She's calling herself 'Desyrel' after the pills Ralph takes. Says she likes him better on them."

"This, too, shall pass."

"People know nothing whatsoever about bringing up children."

"Evidently not nothing enough to make them stop."

"I'm having an opinion. So are you."

"*Ça bouge,*" Jameson crooned, as the first thrust was felt. "Let me go read the takeoff."

THRUST. Drag. Lift. Gravity.

Dead reckoning. Pilotage.

I remember many things. We're taking off.

Whereupon aeronautics, an abstraction she connected in her charged mind with impulse, extravagance, drive theory, glamour, panache, the firmament, navigation, weather, traffic, histrionics, calculation, cigarettes, alcohol, exit options, anticipation, and memory, took over, assuming the responsibility for her safe delivery.

For the first time in my life, I'm not afraid.

We're climbing: we're ascending over Doheny, Jameson Drive, Waverly, Wayfaring, Silver Lake, Echo Park, Glendale, Pasadena. . . . The lights: look at the lights!

They were flying beyond the zone of glare, over the San Gabriel Mountains.

The moon. "You can't even trust the man in the moon." What is that? I'll remember.

"Miss Wayfaring, here's a pillow. You'll be more comfortable if you want to get some shut-eye."

"Oh, thank you, Kyle. And what are you doing this evening?"

"Screening *Avenged.*"

"You're kidding!"

"Can't help myself, especially with you on board."

"I get it: life and the imitation of life, eh?"

"Motion pictures are not an imitation of life, Miss Wayfaring, they are another life."

131

Suddenly she was singing, "With a song in my heart /
Heaven opens its port-holes to me!"

"Huh?"

"I used to sing it that way: when I was four."

"It takes on a new meaning."

"Doesn't everything, in time?"

"Stretch out and get some shut-eye."

"Or else I may start to hallucinate."

"No, don't do that."

"All right, I won't. Nighty-night."

"Nighty-night, Miss Wayfaring."

"And, Kyle?"

"Yes?"

"This is the life."

"Yes, Miss Wayfaring, I suppose it is."

"This is *it:* you heard it here."

SOMEWHERE halfway in slumber, become, while staying
herself then, herself back when, young Désirée Von
Gelsen and her dead aunt Thalia Bridgewood, she heard
the song in full: a peculiar lullaby.

Go to sleep, you gorgeous little rascal,
Thank your lucky stars you've got a bed;
You better get your shut-eye while the gettin' is good,
You've got some tough nights ahead. . . .
You'll grow up and find it's all a racket,
Cards are stacked against you from the start;
Us gals have got to take it from the time that we're born,
Because we're born with a heart. . . .
You're only a doll, and a man will have you crying too
  soon,

'Cause, after all, you can't even trust the man in the moon.
Go to sleep and dream about your charger . . .
Mmm-a-mmm-a-mmm-a-mmm-a-mmm . . .
Sir Galahad is waiting—a mmm-a-mmm . . .

Jameson O'Maurigan returned from the flight deck to find Kaye Wayfaring fast asleep. Sitting opposite, he kept the watch.

SHE LAY in her sickbed in the nursery, upstairs in the house on Jefferson Street in Milledgeville. Two black women, Pye and Doe, were hanging freshly laundered muslin curtains with cartoon animals sewn on floating at various angles, and a third, her favorite, Sumpsie, was sitting next to the sickbed, having parted the netting, feeding her nutmeg custard, and saying, "You and yoah bruthuh, child, you are woise than one anothuh!" She listened to her brother Jackson, locked in the round turret room above. "Horse shit! Dawg shit! Ape shit! Rabbit shit! Cat shit! Rat shit! Bat shit! *Elephant* shit!" Pye and Doe laughed so hard they fell off the ladder into the curtains and through the open window, whereupon Sumpsie jumped up and leaped out after them, howling, "Them *coytins* is jest bin *wawshed!*"

She felt the nutmeg go straight to her head and lift her out of the sickbed. After circling the room, she drifted out the window and hovered over the lawn like a child-shaped helium balloon, while, below, Pye, Doe, and Sumpsie were rolling around on the trim grass, involved in the circus-animal curtains, while Thalia Bridgewood, Margaret Mitchell Marsh, Ruth Draper, and Kaye's aunt Dorothy Wayfaring Bridgewood, her cousins Gabriel and Clayton's mother, swooped about like Disney's dancing pachyderms in picture hats, wielding croquet mallets and braying, "Cordelia, one of your children is loose!"

She floated past the turret window, thumbing her nose at her brother inside.

"Worm shit! Fly shit! *Aardvark* shit!" he screamed at her.

She floated up over the turret and hovered above the roof.

"Cordelia! Cordelia!" the white women were calling.

"Miz Coadelia, that child she flyin' *away!*" the black women cried.

Where's my mother anyway? Kaye Wayfaring asked. Doesn't she give a rat's ass?

Whereupon the floating child willed herself sucked into the chimney.

"Miz Coadelia, she di*sappeah*ed now: she *goan!*" the black women wailed in chorus on the lawn.

Crouched in the fireplace of the master bedroom, she heard the commotion outside.

She doesn't care. Where is she?

In the dressing-table mirror, she saw herself covered with soot.

Where is she? Got to find her. She's sitting somewhere taking her heat medicine.

She opened the door and stepped into the long, dark hall. At the far end, the door to the sewing room, ajar, reflected flat white light. As she came closer, she heard her mother's singing voice. The same old song.

> *Once in a lifetime love comes your way,*
> *Once in a lifetime it really comes to stay;*

When you discover the stars are just right,
And somebody whispers, "I'm lonesome tonight."
Once in a blue moon the waiting ends,
And 'neath a new moon, you take what heaven sends;
Two arms around you, so glad that they've found you;
Once in a lifetime, dear.

Cordelia Bridgewood Wayfaring turned around to address her errant daughter.

"What is it yoah aftuh, Miss, creatin' this histrionic commotion?"

"Want to go home."

"Home? We awh home on Jeffuhson Street in Milledgeville, neah the banks of thuh lugubrious Oconee, in the house of yoah Aunt Theodora, known to the world at large as 'Thalia' Bridgewood, stauh of the New York stage and network radio. Home is wheah the familuh is. Weah home."

"Home to Clayton."

"You and that othuh Cherokee ridgerunnuh in theah! What you both cleahly fancy doin' is skunkin' up and down Woahwomun Dell all summuh long, chewin' on ropes of licorice: nothin' else!"

"So?"

"So, Miss Wayfarin', you and Mistuh Wayfarin'—who is, by the way, yoah *bruthuh* and not, as you keep insistin', yoah husband—a husband vereh incidentalleh bein' an entiteh I consideh you vereh unlikeleh *evuh* to *snayuh*—you and Mistuh Wayfarin' are sadly down on yoah luck!"

"Shit."

"You do and you wipe it up. Ahm not impressed."

"Fuck."

"Loveleh! We'll jest put you on network radio with yoah equalleh enchantin' sibling."

"I hate the sonavabitch."

"Look at huh standin' theah, black as a crow and twice as malicious!"

"What's *m'lishus?*"

"You may well go on down to Foat Goahdun and ask yoah fathuh. When Ah think how happy I was carryin' you, and now *this:* I could go back to Clayton mahself tomorrow and just throw mahself into Hawthorne's Pool at the Tallulah Gorge, the entryway to thuh undehworld!"

"Miz Coadelia! Miz Coadelia, no!"

She woke with a start as the aircraft hit an air pocket and was knocked about in the sky.

"Are you all right?" Jameson asked, from across the tilting cabin.

"My mother took her own life."

"Dreaming about it again?"

"Not about it: about the unhappiness that led up to it."

"Fasten your seatbelt, please, I'm going to check up front."

"I'd check down back behind the galley, if I were you. I don't think that picture ought to be screened at certain altitudes."

"There's some indication of storm activity coming down from Canada."

"Tell the guys to navigate with care. I've got something I'm supposed to deliver back East."

"No more bad dreams, then, O.K.?"

"Don't be Irish: dreams are dreams."

"I'm a man: what do I know?"

" 'The heart of man, without being such a hopeless laby-

rinth as the heart of woman, is still sufficiently compli-
cated.' "

They entered a corridor of increased turbulence.

"Fasten that thing, would you please? I'll be right back."

"Could you see if anyone up there has a piece of licorice,
and bring it back here with you?"

MAWRDEW CZGOWCHWZ, up early, watched the already
heavy snow falling on Gramercy Park. Pigeons gurgled in
the wainscoting, and sparrows landed in the leafless
branches of the district's trees.

Oriole, Bluejay, and Thrasher: off Doheny. Odd, the
things you remember.

What is in flower out there?

It's true, all right: I want her here where I can keep an
eye on her.

Unlikely, the telephone rang.

Of all the— Who in the world? She carefully uncradled
the solarium extension.

"*Pronto.*"

"*Pronto? Pronto,* is it? Have I reached by mistake the
Supreme Macaroni Company?" the Countess Madge
O'Meaghre Gautier cooed at the other end of the line.

"One takes certain precautions," Mawrdew Czgowchwz
replied. "What on earth are you doing up, for example,
before the break of noon?"

"I've been on the line since *dawn!* The Tillinghast
woman called from the South Fork to confess her sleepless-
ness and apprehension about making it to the festivities
tonight, whereupon another saga crackled down the wire,
whereafter the venerable Chimère, ne Čechách, rang up:

Did I think the snow would prevent the show, because he's had an oracular dream that *Garbo* is going to appear at the front door in a Hispano-Suiza, swathed in ermine and encased in jet beads. I said, 'It's your dream, darling, but it doesn't much resemble the Garbo I saw yesterday at the bank.' New York, New York!"

"Indeed, and won't it be lovely when they get it built."

"Any word from your crowd, then?"

"I reckon they're on their way."

"From the opposite ends of the continent!"

"Ever the romantic you."

"And you?"

"I remember that voyages were a great aphrodisiac, but these days I prefer to sit in one place and watch snow fall."

"Now, isn't that a darlin' thing to utter for posterity!"

"Oh, go sit on your posterity, you iniquitous old Carmelite!"

"Is your heat up? I'm sittin' here freezing me arse off."

"Well, put the phone down and go push up your thermostat."

"I'm mortally terrified of that contraption altogether. Sean Darragh always sets it, and where is he at the moment only snug and warm in a jet plane somewhere over the Continental Divide. Anyway, what are you wearing to this shindig tonight?"

"I haven't decided. I thought I might sport ermine and jet beads."

"I'm going to hang up and go put me stove on. Don't forget we're on for that Dakota lunch."

"I shall somehow manage to crawl through the snow to sit amongst you."

"I must say that in addition to being one of the greatest *artistes* of our time, you have been a social saint about town for as long as anyone can recall."

"You're too kind: you always were. Go turn on your oven."

"And this time next year you'll be makin' a proper *dote* of a grandma—and then you can sit and look at snow and tell stories and prove that adage of Victoria's about the bells and the procession. Toodle-oo, darlin'!"

No pot tocar carilon y andar a la procesión.

She saw in her mind's eye a procession through the snow.

Où sont les neiges. There is no this time next year. Things as they are. Posterity.

The telephone rang again.

"Yes? Oh, hello. Have you been up all night? Of course you have. . . . Of course she did. What? Deliverance. Well, and why not? . . . I will if I get the chance. . . . I get the chance in no time. I quite agree: she's a determined woman. . . . I don't know: I don't presume. . . . I wasn't married either. Your father insisted: it was the fifties. . . . You're not. No, I am not surprised: I didn't think you would, really: it isn't your sort of occasion. . . . She did. Yes, he'll be there, I'm sure: it's very much his sort of occasion. . . . He looks like you when he scowls, in those publicity photographs. Anything else? Yes, I'll keep an eye on her. I know I did: I well remember the afternoon: something whispered to me. . . . Go take a nap, she'll be telephoning when they land. . . . I rather imagine she's fast asleep, unless she's still taken up with divination. Go take a nap."

. . .

RETURNING from the toilet, Kaye Wayfaring glanced at *Avenged* on the screen affixed to the bulkhead behind the galley. There was Candace herself, off at a gallop across the Sheep Meadow, plotting and replotting her weird, obsessive revenge (in heavy-lidded, sloe-eyed relentless close-up, looking pummeled, looking dredged).

"Do you think it's of our time?" she asked the steward, who sat belted in the upright position, smoking a Marlboro, watching.

He looked up at her through wet, red eyes. "It's of all time."

MAWRDEW CZGOWCHWZ sat at the kitchen table, drinking her morning coffee and looking into Deliverance in the *I Ching*.

THE JUDGMENT
DELIVERANCE. *The southwest furthers.*
If there is no longer anything where one has to go,
Return brings good fortune.
If there is still something where one has to go,
Hastening brings good fortune.
THE IMAGE
Thunder and rain set in:
The image of DELIVERANCE.
Thus the superior wo(man) pardons mistakes
And forgives misdeeds.

Winter Meeting

A thunderstorm has the effect of clearing the air; the superior wo(man) produces a similar effect when dealing with mistakes and sins of wo(men) that induce a condition of tension. Through clarity s(he) brings deliverance. However, when failings come to light, s(he) does not dwell on them; s(he) simply passes over mistakes, the unintentional transgressions, just as thunder dies away. S(he) forgives misdeeds, the intentional transgressions, just as water washes everything clean.

THE LINES
Six at the beginning means:
Without blame.

In keeping with the situation, few words are needed. The hindrance is past, deliverance has come. One recuperates in peace and keeps still. This is the right thing to do in times when difficulties have been overcome.

Nine in the second place means:
One kills three foxes in the field
And receives a yellow arrow.

(That's the Oscar, it must be, although there are five nominations.)

Perseverance brings good fortune.

. . . The obstacles in public life are the designing foxes who try to influence the ruler through flattery. They must be removed before there can be any deliverance.

. . . If one is devoted wholeheartedly to the task of deliverance, s(he) develops so much inner strength from rectitude that it acts as a weapon against all that is false and low.

(She isn't going to like hearing about her rectitude. These things must be managed delicately . . . delicately. . . .)

> *Six in the third place means:*
> *If one carries a burden on the back*
> *And nonetheless rides in a carriage,*
> *S(he) thereby encourages robbers to draw near.*
> *Perseverance leads to humiliation.*

(The burden's in front, not back. No riding in carriages — Mmn—check. Probably means she must give up the screen for a time. *No pot tocar carilon y andar en la procesión.*)

> *Nine in the fourth place means:*
> *Deliver yourself from your great toe.*
> *Then the companion comes,*
> *And him you can trust.*

(Where have I heard that before? "Darling, get over yourself." That must be conveyed *very* delicately. . . .)

In times of standstill it will happen that inferior people attach themselves to a superior wo(man), and through force of daily habit they may grow very close and become indispensable. . . . But when the time of deliv-

142

erance draws near, with its call to deeds, a wo(man) must go out free from such chance acquaintances with whom s(he) has no inner connection. For otherwise the friend(s) . . . on whom s(he) could really rely and together with whom s(he) could accomplish something, mistrust. . . .

(It is perfectly true. Jacob is a volatile, jealous, and possessive man, as was his father. It is as poor Roland said: In any man who utters the other's absence, something feminine is declared: this man who waits and who suffers is miraculously feminized. A man is not feminized because he is inverted, but because he is in love. The future will belong to the subjects in whom there is something feminine. *C'est ça.*)

> *Six in the fifth place means:*
> *If only the superior wo(man) can attain to*
>   *self-deliverance,*
> *It brings good fortune.*
> *Thus s(he) proves to inferior wo(men) that s(he) is in*
>   *earnest.*

Times of deliverance demand inner resolve. Inferior people cannot be driven off by prohibitions or any external means. If one deserves to be rid of them, one must first break completely with them in one's own mind; they will see for themselves that s(he) is earnest and will withdraw.

(They can mail her the Oscar.)

Six at the top means:
The prince(ss) shoots at a hawk on a high wall.
S(he) kills it. Everything serves to further.

The hawk on a high wall is the symbol of a powerful inferior in a high position who is hindering the deliverance. . . . S(he) must be forcibly removed, and this requires appropriate means.

(I must supplant the mother, Cordelia. That is all there is to it.)

"Look, here's the shot," Kaye whispered to Jameson. "Feet, legs, torso, face: hounded down by torment: driven to distraction."

"The camera her accuser."

"I had just finished reading the letter. I collapsed at the fountain, he called 'Cut,' and then we went together and sealed the letter up in the tunnel wall."

"And you wondered whether Jacob would come back the next afternoon."

"We've crossed the agonic line, haven't we?"

"Yes, and we'll be landing in Atlanta."

"Weather. Traffic."

"What?"

"Nothing—just a memory."

"It may clear up later on."

"Whatever. Ariadne."

"The way out is the way in."

"The way up is the way down."

"You are *good* in this picture!"

. . .

EXECUTIVE at her Sheraton writing desk in the front parlor, looking out the long windows at the snow now blanketing Gramercy Park, Mawrdew Czgowchwz followed the *I Ching*'s commentary on the Deliverance hexagram, considering its application to the Kaye Wayfaring situation.

> . . . In one aspect, this hexagram is a further development of the situation described in Chun, DIFFICULTY AT THE BEGINNING. . . . In terms of the Image, thunder —electricity—has penetrated the rain clouds. There is release from tension. The thunderstorm breaks, and the whole of nature breathes freely again.

(Difficulty at the beginning. It's always the beginning. The ache, the fear, the new life: the fear for the new life: the fear of it supplanting. Then, too, the family's curses. The thunderstorm breaks many a time and often within, before the water breaks at last, and the thing is over, and begun. . . .)

THE JUDGMENT
DELIVERANCE. *The southwest furthers.*
If there is no longer anything where one has to go,
Return brings good fortune.
If there is still something where one has to go,
Hastening brings good fortune.

Commentary on the Decision
DELIVERANCE. Danger produces movement.

Through movement one escapes danger: this is deliverance.

During deliverance "the southwest furthers": by going s(he) wins the multitude.

"The return brings good fortune," because s(he) wins the central position.

(There is telluric vexation, or can be, in conceiving for the first time over forty, but that is not it so much as the threat of the dead calling out for a stillbirth. Her movement must continue. The exercises: the breathing: the rest. This is the thing: to concentrate the movement loop in the private circle, the place of light and heat and constant nourishment. . . . The multitude, the audience now have their *Avenged* to look at and to look at. . . . The central position: she: the woman of the house.)

If there is still something . . . hastening brings good fortune.

(What am I getting here? Only another quest, which won't signal. I'm getting strongly that there's someplace she hasn't gone she's got to go. *The going is meritorious.* My will will not . . . Something at the Chimère show? I'm getting something sooner than that, today, which won't signal. . . .)

When heaven and earth deliver themselves, thunder and rain set in. When thunder and rain set in, the seed pods of all fruits, plants, and trees break open.

(Let me get my will out of this, shall I, and see what there is in it, the thing as it is?

The seed pods: where? She's on her way here, now, even as I speak to myself.)

The time of DELIVERANCE *is great indeed.*

. . . The southwest is the place of the trigram K'un, the Receptive. Its opposite, the northeast, is no longer mentioned, because here the difficulties have already been overcome. K'un also means the multitude.

(This is savory enough. The Southwest and the Multitude. She's left them; she's in the air. Unless New York, which is southwest of Manitoy—and the multitude here—but no, New York cannot be at the same time, in the provenance of a single throw, both the Southwest and the Northeast.)

. . . When deliverance has only just come, a certain protection is needed, a quiet nurturing under the maternal care of the Receptive. . . . But it is important to liberate oneself from inferior wo(men) who are also yielding in temperament.

(Yielding into the abyss, leaving behind accusatory diaries. It may become necessary for me to go down to that town deep in her past, with her or without her, before long, to take that document out of the vault, read it, and destroy it. To keep it away from the men who, if they get a look at it, will undoubtedly decide it ought to be made into a scenario for a Hyperion Productions motion picture starring the very Kaye Wayfaring: I know well how their minds work. . . .)

She reviewed every aspect of the situation.

(The conclusion is unmistakable: there has been a shift in the scheme I woke up to. Having left Los Angeles, she's got something to do in a place, an environ southwest of New York, in which some species of multitude is wont to nourish. . . . Look at that snow. . . . how can they— *Numi*, woman, that's it, of course, they can't! Where *are* they? Where will they?)

THEY SAT at a table on the carousel of the Sun Dial Lounge, drinking Coca-Cola and revolving clockwise six degrees a minute in the winter morning sun, above the new Atlanta.

" 'Reach for the ring—keep reaching!' is what the aunt always did say," said Kaye Wayfaring to Jameson O'Maurigan. "Look at all that gold leaf on the dome of the capitol!"

"This is the first of these rooms I've ever been in," said Jameson, looking the city over, checking his pocket compass. "Let me envision the premiere of *Another Day: To-morrow.*"

"Did I ever tell you what the laurel-wreathed war hero Colonel 'Buck'-as-in-pass-it Wayfaring did to his some-swell-decoration daughter when she begged him—as long as they were detouring to Atlanta on the way back to Clayton from Milledgeville—begged him to take her to *Gone With the Wind?* He took her into the lobby of the Grand and spent two hours showing her the lobby cards and telling her the whole story: the book version, as it turned out. . . . She went home to Clayton and told her brother Jackson she'd been to see *Gone With the Wind* at long last—and when she told him how, how he laughed until the piss rolled down his leg, and howled over and over again, 'You *fool!* You *fool!*' And that night the two of them snuck into the rumble seat of the jalopy parked in front of the Clayton Café and rode up to the Paradise Mountain Drive-In and saw through the front windshield —while whoever the hell they were groveled under the dashboard—*Duel in the Sun*. '*That* is what a motion picture is!' he let her know, sharing one of his precious Luckies. They were worse than one another, actually, Buck and his boy."

"Just remember you never wound up in the bins at Milledgeville, or Camarillo, or any other resort they planned to send you to for rest and recreation after your tour of duty."

"Milledgeville is down there," Kaye observed, stretching out her left arm. "She was first hospitalized in Milledgeville just after the war. Clayton is up there," she said, extending her right arm.

"Hold that attitude of surrender: it's becoming."

"The only thing I'm becoming is hungry, angry, lonely, and exhausted."

"That's four things. Want to take a morning nap in your natal city?"

"I probably should, for the child's sake, but I have no desire to resume dreaming till I'm safely bedded down with my accomplice."

"Los Angeles is over there," Jameson remarked, pointing thumb crooked over his left shoulder.

"How would you like to drive me to Clayton?" Kaye suddenly asked.

"What, now?"

"Yes, we could get there by lunch."

"You miss the food: a craving."

"You could say that."

"You could sing it if you had a tune to it."

"It just came to me this second. I was remembering a road sign on Highway Four forty-one. 'Do Not Drive In Breakdown Lane,' and some kind of voice told me to get on the road and drive right to the bank to get my mother's diary out of the vault. With you with me, I know I can do that much. You understand, don't you?"

"I'm your other accomplice."

"It's true, you are—but you'd certainly rather be relaxing."

"This is exciting, and excitement is relaxing. If weather conditions clear up North, they can come and collect us."

"Let me go make two phone calls."

"Tell one of them I love him—and direct him will he kindly meet the ferry day after tomorrow."

Mawrdew Czgowchwz passed up the coffee and liqueurs and went to call her son on Manitoy.

"Hello there, this is your mother in New York. I think you would testify that I never do this kind of thing—nevertheless— What? Atlanta. . . . Of course. Atlanta's the logical landing. To where? To Clayton. But why? . . . The Tallulah Gorge?"

The Countess Madge O'Meaghre Gautier had followed Mawrdew Czgowchwz into the library of Consuelo Gilligan's apartment in the Dakota.

"The Gilligan has just put on her conical cap—claims to have foreseen the whole clamor in its manifest particulars, and moreover— I fled the auditorium. What's going on?"

"Atlanta. Clayton. Tallulah Gorge. What? No, dear, I was only repeating: for your deaf auntie from the East Side."

The co-auditor advanced. "I'll take that phone, if you please. . . . Hello, how are you? What, would you tell me, is this whole thing ever about? Hmmm . . . So . . . Hmmm . . . So . . . Hmmm . . . So."

Mawrdew Czgowchwz walked to the library door. "I think I will have a little something after all. Tell him not to worry: it will all be resolved before midnight."

"You stay right here! What? No, not you, darlin', your mother. Don't worry, it's all goin' to be resolved before midnight."

The Countess handed the telephone back to Mawrdew Czgowchwz, who, having crossed back, stood looking out the window at Central Park.

"Hello, again. Don't worry. I just heard thunder out the window. . . . Yes, I worked it out myself this morning, and again with Madge at Magwyck before we came over here to lunch. Before lunch Consuelo had a go, and is, as you have heard, in there now, starting all over from scratch: which itch you know. . . . I *am* being serious, and I realize this is your life. . . . Well, you *could* get on a train. . . . I expect she'll make the show, then Magwyck, then home with me in a taxi. The train gets in at half past three, and you know the way from Penn Station. All right, if you like, yes, I think that's what you ought to do. . . . Yes, well, just remember, your mother wore army boots. All right, get a move on. Bye."

"Good on you: it's about time!" the Countess Madge declared.

"But I don't *do* things like that!" Mawrdew Czgowchwz announced.

"There are things you just don't do until you do," her closest friend declared with finality.

"What do you say we make our excuses and go looking at hats?" sighed the mother-in-spite-of-herself.

"Ah, now there's a thing. Where are the hats of . . ."

"Look, the rain's come!"

Clayton, Georgia
January on the wane

My dearest Mawrdew Czgowchwz,

This for your eyes before we meet and dance a round at the event of the season (providing the errant we achieve the metropolis in time to put in an appearance).

The Wayf lies sleeping in an upstairs room, while here in front of a spark-spitting cedar log fire (having risen from a deal spindle-back chair where I'd been perched looking across at the oldest living being in north Georgia, a Miss Bama Eula Bridgewood, formerly of Spoiled Cane Creek, White County: the Wayf's great-aunt, a maiden lady, as she nods away, perhaps involved in a negotiation with eternity's preceptors), this living I, your poet, settled to work at the cherry escritoire, makes one more bold attempt to tell his living muse what-all what-for, in time.

We were breakfasting in a revolving solarium some-where in the sky over Atlanta, and she was looking sun-child radiant, carefree, and not a day over thirty-one, when suddenly as if black lightning had just torn the face of the morning sky, one of those Gemini bisect frowns com-menced to rearrange the left side of her face, and under-neath what she said she said "the way out is the way in."

On the way out of Atlanta, we stopped to visit a grey nun: a nun with a name like anybody else: a nun the Wayf had gone to for particular instruction at a time when she was called Diana and the nun a man's name I disremember. I took a walk outside in the enclosed grove of denuded oleanders, and through open windows I could hear the two of them laughing, and the Wayf chanting "Dear Saint Ann, get me a man, quick as you can!" The whole thing made me nervous.

We took the Interstate, and then the old road that runs up to Clayton from Milledgeville and from Athens: all those sacred groves of memory Bridgewood used to go on, on and *on* about. It was a calm drive all told, even if Miss made me a little edgy now and again singing to an old hillbilly tune a song she had made up with the brother when they were children, a song based on a road sign: DO NOT DRIVE IN BREAKDOWN LANE—an alarmingly precocious song. But what of that: weren't we all, I said to myself.

We pulled over at Tallulah Gorge, some distance to Clayton. She paid the way in and walked directly to one of those heart-shaped chrome telescope devices you put a quarter in: which she did, and focused the lens down to eleven degrees, straight between the split rails of a guard fence. "Look down there: see what you see." Which I did, and saw a great rock formation, a cascade, a rock pool, a roaring river: and I heard her telling me, "When I would sit up on the flat rock and look over at the cascade they'd installed for the picture: how it spilled over the rocks down the Gill and out into the lake, I'd see this gorge. She used to take us here: Jackson, Gabriel and me, and point down and tell us the story of the three billy goats and the troll. Over there is where she jumped." And she flipped the telescope up to ninety degrees to show me the flat table rock just across the gorge.

Our next stop was at the bank. A brand new glass and

boulder affair on the highway at the bottom of the hill the town sits on. She was in and out in as short a time as you would take on Park Avenue South to make a quick withdrawal from the mouth in the wall: carrying the diary that Cordelia left behind. It's been years and years, I said to myself: why now: why this afternoon with me? (I am no grave of secrets, only progressively become disinclined to fly telling colors. And yet from time to time she has the brass to say "I see through you.")

The mood lifted as she directed me out Warwoman Road past an American Legion Hall and a sign pointing toward a Camp Pinnacle, into the Warwoman Dell, through which she led me with some care, to examine certain specific trees: a whip tree, a sycamore, a post oak, in among the frequencies of pine. I wondered at such a homing instinct, but she said in the thaw after the early January rains it wasn't very difficult. "Look at that," she said, "seed pods bursting open. Tell her." I'm telling you. "In summer the dell gets all covered over by a terrible Japanese creeper called a kudzu vine that grows a foot a night. The old bastard used to tell us that if we slept out —especially together—it would get us around the neck and crawl up our orifices. I looked it up. He was terribly imaginative in his cups. He utterly despised Clayton. She'd get grand and say Clayton was where all the original Bridgewoods were raised, and he'd say back 'That they were indeed, until the rope broke.' "

In People's Department Store, quite a to-do. She walked up to the woman overseeing yard goods and said right out, "Where was Franklin Pangborn?" The woman blinked and opened her mouth wide—then shut it right away and snapped, "On Sydney Greenstreet." Then without pause, the Wayf: "Why did Myrna Loy?" "Cawse Mary Asta!" Whereupon they fell into one another's embrace. (I inspected the neckties, but found myself unable to make a purchase decision.) "We won the bathtub derby together in 1954!" the reunited cohorts let the stranger know.

We drove up to something called the Nacoochee School, which the brother had attended while your woman was with the grey nuns in Atlanta, and then back through the town and up a winding road to the no-longer-operative Bridgewood's Hotel. (I heard voices in the trees retelling all Thalia's old boarder stories.) We spoke a word to Thalia's cousin colonel's widow, a younger member of Miss Bama's generation, and her daughter, who assured the former denizen of Warwoman Dell and sometime upstairs maid of work and general dogsbody, "Saw you up theah on that screen. Lahked whut we sawh."

They are remodeling Main Street, taking out the tupelos and replacing them with what the woman at People's called "shrubs in tubs."

The Wayf looked up at the deco Clayton Café sign and said, "I suppose that'll go before long." She wondered how, if she were to play Cordelia's diary on the screen, the town would take to Orphrey having it reconstructed exactly as it was in 1941, tupelos and all. And that and the walking succeeded in making her feel beat enough to kip.

Which brought us back to this room.

I've perused the diary. I understand what she means when she says a thing like "There were times when I became convinced I'd never been born at all—that I was just one of my mother's hangovers." She asked me to let her know what I thought of its—the diary's—filmic possibilities—still half-teasingly, I thought, until she said

"Czgowchwz played her mother pregnant while pregnant herself with the twins: it's an intriguing thing to think about doing, don't you think?" I didn't think: I was scared out of my wits. Just before retiring she repeated the following story . . . Sometime in the early forties, Cordelia had decided to pay an impromptu visit to New York to check up on her sister, the toast of the Rialto. Apparently played the whole north Georgia angle very indicatively—up to the point where, at a hastily convened cocktail matinee, the hijinks and shenanigans moved Goodwife Cornell, the neighbor, to corner New York's premiere comedienne in her efficiency kitchen overlooking the East River just long enough to blurt out (in the hearing of guests queuing to relieve themselves of urgent bladders excited by suppressed hysterics): "Bridgewood, we knew you were a woman entirely without principle—but to go and hire that character woman off Sixth Avenue, bring her in here, and introduce her as your *sister!*"

"She went and made a county-talk of herself," the oulwen in the rocker said after the Wayf had left—and she was talking not about the mother Cordelia's daughter Diana Kaye's career on the screen—a thing she didn't seem to find in the least interesting—but of the life career of the daughter's mother, of whom she had earlier, in company, hissed out the opinion, "Girl, yoah momma was *the* ringtail bitch of Rabun County, make no mistake and no excuse!" Altogether Cordelia seems to have been material for one of Draper's lost monologues—subject to further research, but no subject, I promise you faithfully, for your woman upstairs. So far as my collaborating: I wouldn't touch it with tongs. . . .

I sat alone with Miss Bama Eula Bridgewood, hoping to

elicit more information about the Wayf's childhood—al-though I think I know enough for any sympathist—but most of what the Ancient of Days told me was about herself, and I think were you here with me you'd agree that each of us has had sufficient traffick in our Irishry with like crones, whose histories we do part cherish, part abhor.

"Listen for the whipporwill" is her watchword. She was born in 1885 out in Wyoming somewhere, where some of the Easters and Bridgewoods had wandered after the Civil War. "Fust Wayfarins we evuh come acrost we come acrost in Nevada—befoah they wuz tuhned back t' Califor-nia t' rape, rob, an' murdeh moah innacent people. That wuz jest the way they wuh, them Wayfarins, and theah wuz no stoppin' 'em."

The Wayf likes to entertain her in conversation in order to hear bits like "We had t' frail ouah grain with a doal, and saved the tops off corn foah winteh feed." Says it reminds her of the lyrics "Mairzy doats and dozy doats and little lambsy divy," and "Hut sut rawlson on the rillerah and a brawla brawla suet."

Winter was quilt-making time. They made featherbeds and pillows out of duck and chicken feathers. The father made shoes from cowhide, and during long winter after-noons they picked out black walnuts with a crochet hook. Gathered around a cozy fire, they caught up with their chores. . . . It is plain to me that the Wayf connects such images with the increase of pregnancy, and draws comfort from the as yet quasi-fictive projection of her life to come, in February, on Manitoy. Mountain people, the Wayf re-calls, and Miss Bama Eula affirms, enjoyed getting up early, seeing the sun rise, and feeling the fresh dew's shiny drops. I assured her she could indeed by giving up staying up afford herself the delirious ecstasy of getting up. . . .

There were panthers on Unicoi Mountain, at Spoiled Cane Creek, and in Warwoman Dell in those days—no more, says Miss Bama Eula Bridgewood. "No more panthers," quoth the Wayf, "but memories ready to spring off any shelf indoors or out and rip your insides out." "Meadow muffins!" quoth the crone. "You got to let yoah memorehs know who's in charge around heah, that's awl!" She concluded the interview with a wrap-up in two parts. "Age comes, the bodeh withuhs, and the mand is free t' wanduh solitareh." "Ah reckon a refrigeratuh is the closes' thing theah is to a hawt. It sets theah awl deh an' awl naht awl yeah long, and you don't know nuthin' till it stops woikin—then you fahnd out."

The Rabun County police, in collaboration with the Georgia state troopers, have kindly let me know that they will gladly put at Miss Wayfaring's disposal as soon as she wakes, one of the helicopters they regularly employ to ferret out the illegal distillers of ardent spirits in this corner of creation, the better to facilitate her journey back to Atlanta, and, as they have had encouraging word at air traffic control of the clearing of skies in the North, to New York City, where I shall see to it that this missive is put in no other hands but yours, direct from these, those of your ever faithful lieutenant,

Sean Darragh

AT THE Chimère show, the sideshow was getting all the attention. They were ringed four deep along the darkened oval chamber's walls, looking into the hologram and serving remarks.

"In Wayfaring's face are many possible faces."

"Mawrdew Czgowchwz. Detractors used to say she had a wobble you could walk through, and now you can walk through her image."

"Hers and Kaye Wayfaring's sitting together, talking."

"Can we talk?"

"Kaye Wayfaring set to play Mawrdew Czgowchwz in *The Mawrdew Czgowchwz Story*—can it be? Where will Orphrey Whither find the scratch?"

"For almost four decades, Orphrey Whither has bubbled fools out of their goods and cash dollars to make moompix: he'll raise it."

"Where is Whither anyway?"

"Orphrey is on location."

"Is there *another* picture in the *works?*"

"I wouldn't know, darling. Orphrey is on location wherever he tarries."

"And the real Mawrdew Czgowchwz and the real Kaye Wayfaring will be *here* at any moment."

In Folâtre's long gallery, the photographer Chimère (né Čechách) ventilated to his assistant Dalibor, the hair designer Cégèste, and his assistant Georgie.

"The fabulous of forty seasons are hanging on these walls. Their glances bear evidence! And where is everybody? Inside, captivated by technology."

"Ever eager to embrace the upcoming, Maestro, you have endorsed holography, ennobling it!" Dalibor judiciously rejoined.

"Alors, mon pauvre Cégèste, la vie s'en roule . . . s'en roule!"

"C'est ça; tant pis. Dites-moi, mon vieux—où sont les négligées d'antan?"

"Flambeur! Tu te moque de moi!"

"*Pas du tout, je suis absolument sincère—toujours sincère,
toujours fidèle.*"

"The upsweep always decides," Georgie remarked,
studying a photograph of Mawrdew Czgowchwz taken in
nineteen forty-nine.

"Decides what, my poor darling?" the photographer
asked.

"The rest of the look—the glance."

"In another minute," Chimère declared, "I am going in
there and pulling the plug on that scintillating attraction!"

"It's a night to run outdoors!" Dalibor announced. "The
snow has stopped, the rain has stopped. . . . A bright white
moon—"

"My poor darling, please, you stop," Chimère decreed.
"I go inside, I pull the plug. I tell them when Madame
Czgowchwz and Miss Wayfaring themselves arrive, then
we play hologram again!"

"If I were you, I wouldn't hold my shutter open,"
snapped Goneril Dreene, passing by. "Hot rumor has it
Wayfaring has disappeared—gone back to the Land of
Oz."

"Drunk and distasteful woman!" Chimère hissed in the
reporter's wake.

"I heard some things this afternoon *I* didn't care for,"
Georgie admitted, crossing and standing in front of a photograph of Kaye Wayfaring taken in nineteen seventy-
nine.

"The things, I could tell you," Cégèste averred, "that fall
out of some people's hair when it's let down . . ."

THROUGH the port windows of the descending Phaeton,
Kaye Wayfaring saluted the great nocturnal New York

skyline blazing against a blue-black satin winter sky, and, comparing its vertical signature to the horizontal signature of Los Angeles, told herself with conviction she had at last arrived at home from home.

THE CROWD at Folâtre had become restive.

"That's when I *knew*—you would have, too."

"*Ebbene, s'è vero, dovrebbe* non *essere!*"

"*Ich hoffe das es ihnen nichts schlecht geht. . . .*"

"I prefer a picture of a tree to a tree. Does that give you a problem?"

"I *hate the* dance!"

"We're talking *angry woman!*"

"That's what I said, bub, tough love."

"*Polished,* as it were, by pain . . .*"

"*Open sin?*"

"*Nostalgia in Chromium*— she'd be perfect!"

"Yes, like the prophet Jeremiah, he has loved strangers and walked after them. . . ."

Rumors concerning the whereabouts of Kaye Wayfaring and Mawrdew Czgowchwz—it was being boldly held that the former had succeeded in some significantly untoward way in detaining the latter—had ripened into accusation under the hot lamp of celebrity inquisition.

"It is one of the marks of this dim age," one impatient demi-rep complained out loud to Philander Dreene, "that the tantrums of celluloid *eidola* are deemed fit for adult conversation!"

"Excuse me for butting in, Sister," Georgie, overhearing, barked, "but how would you like a fat lip to go with the rest of that ugly face you wore here tonight to astonish the populace?"

"Georgie!" Claudia gasped from behind the bar.

"I don't care, Claudia—they can throw me out, but nobody but *nobody* talks about Miss Wayfaring that way!"

"I beg your pardon," the demi-rep gurgled, "what allows you the right to assume that I was referring to your Miss Wayfaring?"

"You were referring maybe to *your* Mary Pickford?" Georgie countered boldly.

"I think you had better stop," the bartender Claudia advised the offender, as Philander Dreene, attracting his sister Goneril's attention, slithered out of the combat zone, "before more of a repercussion occurs than a person in your condition can handle without peer support."

Before the lines of action and reaction in the fracas at the bar could be drawn to greater consequence, a soundless trumpet heralding the arrival of a stellar entity informed the mob that Mawrdew Czgowchwz had come in.

"Look at her, manifesting that winged quality," an itinerant whispered to Goneril Dreene. "Is that Wayfaring's significant other she's got with her?"

"No, it's the brother. Wayfaring's *amor fatal* never leaves the island of Manitoy."

"He's gorgeous, too—whose is *he?*" the itinerant, leering, asked the embittered correspondent.

"Hard to say," cackled Goneril Dreene. "They're a close-knit family."

Chimère approached the diva. Stepping back, he executed a profound bow. "Madame Czgowchwz!"

"Vaclav! *Dobrý večer.* This *is* a celebration!"

"That you did come!"

"Vaclav, *knedlíky*, was Czgowchwz ever a no-show?"

"The public is wondering about Miss Wayfaring."

"She's on her way," replied Tristan Beltane, Mawrdew Czgowchwz's son and redoubtable escort.

"I am greatly relieved to hear it," the photographer rejoined. "Glamour is the primary duty of life: glamour and its maintenance."

"I feel certain," Mawrdew Czgowchwz grandly replied, "that, even as we speak, Miss Wayfaring is seriously occupied with the very rubrics you refer to—although I must tell you that, so far as life's primary maintenance work is concerned, this day's watchword is deliverance."

Kaye Wayfaring closed her mother's diary, fastened the clasp, and turned the key in the lock.

I'm very sorry, lady: I choose not to enter into you.

She picked up the Mawrdew Czgowchwz letter.

47 Gramercy Park
October/an afternoon

My dear Miss Wayfaring,

Yesterday, on an impulse, after a grim look-in on an old haunt, I decided I badly needed to go and look at people *up to* something, and, although I'd told myself in the wake of Sunday's meeting (to which I'd been taken in a closed barouche rumbling over a bridge—someone said Astoria), not to meddle in *Avenged,* there is that about the Ramble venue along the banks of the Gill that—so I put myself up to it and climbed into a hansom at Grand Army Plaza.

As we drew near the set, who should cross the path of the cab, exactly in the manner of the forties (they must use vintage training films based on *Naked City* at the Academy around the block from here to perpetuate a tradition), only this cop whose beat when he was a rookie was around Gramercy Park when the boys were small (which did keep him on the run, I can tell you). "Hello, Madame, you checking out the Wayfaring set?" he inquired, cool as you please, in that way they have of assuming for the occasion they know the correct way of asking an older woman questions about the passing of her days. "But I come up here all the time, Officer Cedrioli, now that the boys are grown up and gone off." (Which was mean, because I know O.C. is good to his mama—as are the boys I'd just referred to, in their way: the elastic.) Blushing, fumbling, he let flap about you—which was straight to the point and terribly moving.

He got very specific. He's worried about you. His fellow officers at the precinct are worried about you. The mounted police are worried about you, and the teller at the First Women's Bank read in Goneril Dreene's "Round-abouts" column in *Pomander Walk* . . . You see why I have no recourse as an Irishwoman of some means and years but to chance my arm and interrupt you at work with my two cents.

What I have to tell you is absolutely terrifying. This too shall pass. Or, as Santayana told Walter Lippmann, who told me while we were dancing together at the Metropolitan Opera House that was on Thirty-ninth Street and Broadway, after that return turn I did in *La Traviata:* "Everything is lyrical in its essence, tragic in its fate, and comic in its existence." (*"Vesti la giubba,"* he seemed to be saying, or was it "Be an existentialist"?) They were for-ever at the ready to offer something uttermostly telling *re* one's lyrical, tragical, and comical—I give you: strong men's scented pieties. So it is with you these days, I fear I hear. (I hear Echo wailing in the wind as she forsakes

Narcissus. They will go on, these narcissists. They will they will they . . .)

I used to sit, look you, on the rock you're most likely sitting on now (if my boy has done his work) reading Francobolli's review of my "elusive" Mélisande, and reading along next to it old Dolores on the correspondences between—I needn't perhaps remind you how wild they all were for what they called *allegory* in the late fifties . . . but now I've quite tripped over the train of thought.

An aside. The Big Z. was going on as Tosca in the late fifties. A rainy night, let's make it. Some kind collegiate supernumerary picked up her velvet gown's torn tail as she was about to sweep on into Sant' Andrea delle Valle . . . "Heh, dun't bother. Dey also pay me here to swip the focking floors." She knew the drill. . . .

I do mind confessing, but I will because it behooves the soul, that I find it difficult always to connect and to reconcile the woman who has rewritten screen history not once but twice in the past decade *(Way Station; We Are Born, We Live, We Die)* with a display of compressed voltage that perturbed the heart's foundations, with that north Georgia hoyden niece of Thalia Bridgewood's who wanted to learn how to sing Puccini's Minnie. ("I only like verismo" were the words you spoke. How very wise you were, my girl, after your own lights.)

The *I Ching* says apropos Oppression: "If one pushes upward without stopping, s(he) is sure to meet with oppression. Oppression means an encounter. . . . Oppression leads to perplexity and thereby to success. . . . Movement brings remorse. If there is remorse, this is an auspicious change." You heard it here, and much good may it do you. (Remember the Countess's tea-leaf reading backstage?)

Therefore and in conclusion (the body of this letter

having clearly slipped through the net), a note concerning the bearer of the remains . . .

When I was forty, and lugging him and his opposite number around in the condition that was referred to at that time as "infanticipating," and all the while doing those turns in Dublin's fair city and environs in Holy Ireland: work released as *Pilgrim Soul*, Orphrey would say "I think we've got what we want," and walk away down the Curragh, and I would see blood all over the earth's floor. In the end the boys got born, the picture done, and I repented me the crook of my contrary ways (especially on Oscar night: always nice to win a prize). But make another picture? Next. It took too much out of me—and it stayed out until that night when . . . The boys, eleven apiece, and gaga over you since that summer they'd worked with you on Manitoy in *Macbeth* (when you taught them to play pinochle and told them that really only boys ought ever play the heroines of Shakespeare), went with me to the Rivoli to see *We Are Born, We Live, We Die.* I walked out of the theater in a daze and said to them, "Your ladyfriend has given it me back." Only to have them shriek like a pair of—what an awkward age they were: "Me back! Me back!" and hobble down Broadway past the great gaping hole in the ground where the Old Met had been, all the way to Madison Square and beyond, acting like two hooligans.

"Mother, what was it Kaye Wayfaring gave you back anyway?" asked the one I'm sending to you today the other afternoon. (He's down from Cambridge, where they've only just recently been pairing *We Are Born, We Live, We Die* with *Way Station*, packing out the Brattle.) What could I say to him now, age that he is? What can I say to *you* except "I think you know," along with the news that neither am I, nor ever was, my favorite piece of information.

And now what's this on the threshing floor? Only the body of the letter after all with the heart of the matter folded roselike and cryptic within. A piece of information: another true confession . . . *Avenged* was the first thing I turned down after *Pilgrim Soul.* As was the case with that one, Orphrey knew what he wanted in the *Dames du Bois de Boulogne* remake, and said he planned to let me know somewhere along the way, but I hadn't the what-all for it (the feeling, yes, the drive, no). I told him he'd have to wait until the boys are at least seven—by which time as it turned out . . . Well, you know what happened that summer on Manitoy. However, even had I made it then with him— and in *that* mood—he'd have made it again with you, and I'd have lost the chance of ever getting back from you . . . You see, I've looked at rushes.

Yes, I have seen the rushes. I am forbidden by the men to tell you so, therefore am thrilled to do same.

I want to tell you not so much that you are doing *it* again, as that you've got them where I think you've wanted them all along. Now do with them what you will. Let them spend their untold millions buying you time. Become avenged. We are not talking about spiteful, withholding behavior that turns in on itself. We are talking performance. Stick to your guns. Fire them. If they come too soon up the hill, fire again and holler if you like "Get off my land!" Let 'em have it in spoonfuls. As Laverne Zuckerman's mother Rhea Esther used to implore in the old days, "You hear me what I'm saying?" If you find a book you like, read it. Stop the music. Do a play. They'll get theirs, you'll see to that; just make sure you get yours.

Candace is your role of roles. You are at the moment the greatest actress in motion pictures. "Miss Wayfaring wears nobody else's old hair."

(Nor, I note with satisfaction, does she call herself an actor.) You're going to deliver. You see, you know what you do . . .

> Your debtor, as then, now and always,
> Mawrdew Czgowchwz

I DO know what I do. Now let me go and talk to her. She knows what's what; that's that.

CLAUDIA was doing M. Girofle a favor by tending the bar at Folâtre.

"Well, Claudia," said Georgie, "she made it. She made it, and she's knocking them dead."

"They came in dead, most of them," the bartender replied. "She's making them feel alive again. A debatable favor."

"I think I know what you mean."

"You know what I mean, all right; don't let anybody else tell you otherwise."

"I'm not crazy about the hair—a little too Rodeo Drive."

"That will fix itself when she gets home. It's a long journey from Malibu to Manitoy."

"You're such a philosopher."

"Georgie, I've been looking after that girl in my mind for years. That girl was hurt bad when young."

"The same goes for most of us, wouldn't you say?"

"Sure it does, but you and I, we've found our salvation in service."

"And she hasn't."

"No. She started out thinking she would. They tell you that. The *Theatuh*. But being histrionic can't save anybody."

"Can love save anybody?"

"What love can save is cab fare and the rent."

"So what you're saying is you save yourself—is that it?"

"What I'm saying is this: If you think you can save yourself the trouble, you can't."

"I don't get it."

"Do me a favor, will you? Bring her this glass of cranberry juice."

"I'll tell her you said hello?"

"Give her my phone number, I'll tell her myself."

"I'll be right back."

"No you won't, Hon—go have yourself a good time."

KAYE WAYFARING, Mawrdew Czgowchwz, Tristan Beltane, and Jameson O'Maurigan, grouped in front of the photographs of Thalia Bridgewood and Marilyn Monroe, talked.

"If we keep talking," said Kaye, "it will be time in no time at all to depart for Magwyck."

"Where they turn the lights down low," said Mawrdew Czgowchwz with delicate emphasis.

"Get up, go out, get seen, go home," said Tristan Beltane. "Some life you go in for, you people."

"You've been sheltered—you'll get yours," said Jameson, nodding pre-emptively at a passerby.

. . .

GEORGIE placed the cranberry juice on a young butler's empty tray. "Please deliver this to Miss Wayfaring, and let her know it's from Claudia, at the bar."

"Which lady's Miss Wayfaring?"

"Very funny, you'll go far—in vaudeville."

"I didn't wear my contacts. They told me to stand in the corner."

"Incredible. Everywhere you go, in the middle of everything, there are people standing in the corner, missing it all."

"If I knew who anybody was, that would make everything worse."

"Only in Manhattan town!"

"Point me in the right direction and I'll do my best."

"I wouldn't want to make anything worse."

"They say she's nice."

"Yes, she's nice. Look, see that group . . ."

"ALL RIGHT, all right, poor darling," Chimère, wringing his hands and rolling his eyes, moaned to M. Girôfle, the gallery intendant. "Plug it back *in!* By all available means, and in every conceivable manner, let the populace be satisfied. Is this not the primary duty of democracy?"

"WHAT is Rumpelstiltskin carrying on about now?" Kaye Wayfaring, sipping her cranberry cocktail, wondered, sotto voce.

The room's mood had grown increasingly edgy, despite

or because of the star's having put in her long-awaited appearance.

"The people have guessed his name—Sensation," said Mawrdew Czgowchwz, "and he's of two minds concerning the resultant fuss."

"He's giving you the Bohemian high sign," Jacob Beltane advised his mother. "What does that mean?"

"It means," said Jameson O'Maurigan, " 'Come stand on my trap door.' "

KAYE WAYFARING and Mawrdew Czgowchwz stood on one side of the laser-illuminated area, while Chimère and Dalibor stood on the other.

"This is the kind of stunt you find recorded in signal diaries of the period," Mawrdew Czgowchwz advised her volatile companion performer.

JAMESON clocked the performance from a vantage point adjacent to the alcove doorway. . . .

The ruby laser hologram of Mawrdew Czgowchwz and Kaye Wayfaring pulsed alive in proper perspective between two parallel mirrors.

Jameson looked across at the legend framed in Plexiglas on the alcove wall.

Matter cannot be precisely located in space and can be shown possibly to exist anywhere, and even everywhere, if it travels at very high speeds.

DO NOT DRIVE IN BREAKDOWN LANE.

They are walking, together.

In everyone's enchanted view, Mawrdew Czgowchwz

and Kaye Wayfaring were seen to enter and transgress their own and one another's atomized imagos.

Chimère, along with his constituents, gasped, repenting the tantrum he'd thrown.

THE CONVERSATION at Magwyck, haunt of the serious-minded, swirled in divers tongues and singular dialect eddies, across thresholds, from room to room.

"In my opinion, that stance is feinting with damned praise."

"I have never understood the meaning of the statement 'She's no better than she should be.'"

"*Clinamen, Tessera, Kenosis, Apophrades*—I woke up."

"So he sent the following message from Western Union: 'Very sorry cannot come—*lie* to *follow.*' He is *one* of a *kind!*"

"Art is long and life is eternal. It's publicity that's brief."

"Always supply, so that there's always supply."

"No, he's an *anti*-elitist. 'The best is the enemy of the good' is what he holds."

"The plain fact is, dear, that if one has ears with which to hear, the birds *do* sing in Greek."

"Struck by lightning in Georgia? No, darling, that was Holly Woodlawn."

"Yes, I saw *him*, but where was the *meal* ticket tonight?"

"Nineteen eighty-four will come and go, just as nineteen *sixty* did!"

THE COUNTESS Madge O'Meaghre Gautier surveyed the room with evident satisfaction.

"It's been another lovely night in New York," Mawr-dew Czgowchwz, standing by the firescreen, informed her fierce conspirator friend, "that ends in due course in this great house."

"Standing here looking at all these together," the Countess replied, "if I close my eyes, I commence hearing the others long gone."

"I've been hearing them all evening. They want in, all right."

"That recumbent creature over there has doubtless been at you with memorial queries."

"The need to know—we knew it once. It overwhelmed us—or nearly."

"What will you tell her: the truth? The whole, long tale?"

"I very much doubt, dear, she'd keep awake throughout the whole, long tale."

"You know my opinion of the notion of that motion picture!"

"Oh, that's just bubble talk. It would end up costing more than anyone's got, except the Vatican."

"I'd not put it past Orphrey Whither to approach the Vatican."

"Nor would I, dear, but I consider it far more likely he'll approach them concerning the sequel to *Gone With the Wind.*"

"I have seen you on the screen, and I don't *want* to see *anyone* playing you on the screen!"

"Never mind me, darling, think of the impossibility of casting you—or Beltane—or the others. Think of *that!*"

"Well . . ."

"I tell you, it was never anything more than a *Schnapps-*

idee. Look at that goddess—the face of fame wreathed in smiles!"

"Nevertheless, you'll tell her."

"I shall accompany your woman to Manitoy tomorrow, deposit her and her friend, and tell them both everything they want to hear. I call that fair, don't you?"

"Interesting. There was a time when you would have said 'everything they need to know' rather than 'everything they want to hear.' "

"There was a time, time out of mind . . ."

"Sure that there was . . ."

"Look, Sean Darragh's getting ready to recite!"

"The way he always used to."

Kaye Wayfaring, comfortably settled in the bagnoire fauteuil, felt the baby kick hard.

They know you're here; they're only being polite. I'll dress you up and bring you back—solemn promise, on the Academy Award.

Out of the corner of her eye, she watched the women watching her and watching Jameson preparing to recite.

Yes, we'll come back; we'll accept the guardians.

Conversation in the room came to a halt as Jameson O'Maurigan's recitation started.

"SESTINA: Recessional . . . Rearrived the gallivants—here, look: the wayfarer / The rhapsode, and the evidence collected./ 'The Southwest furthers.' 'Return brings good fortune.' The song / The old same: things as they are. Particulars. / 'Observe the fast hawk as his wide wings spread.' / I figure out, as does the woman; as does the moon . . .

"Clayton, GA, Warwoman Dell, afternoon: the moon /

174

There and not there: mentor to the wayfarer / Diana. Here crossways: honey-locust seed pods spread / In ripples on the dell floor. They collected / Them when children for fortune-telling: particulars / Of their lives' careers they marked, which they then set to song . . .

"Do Not Drive in Breakdown Lane was the name of the song. / They wrote it together in tree-popping moon / Time—sang it loud in the dead still night. /Particular sorrows were theirs: sorrows of the wayfarer/ Since Genesis: generations' records collected / Played, scratched, replayed, taped scratched, replayed: grievance broadcast spread . . .

"As, eavesdroppers on the porch roof, they, enthralled, lay spread / Eagle, fastened at four corners; NEWS—their song / Played back up at them. Later the yearnings collected / By them sped them on their ways—whereas the moon / Stayed still in the dell, yet followed them. Each wayfarer / Bound away, bade each goodbye: each way particular . . .

"So on, so forth: their destined careers, particulars / Of which we the attentive have heard said, spread / Ballad-like, fashioned legendary. The wayfarer / We know we keep here now, close at home. Her song / Ours now. She the belovèd Diana Kaye: our moon / Our talking-picture star: our revenue collected . . .

" 'The prince shoots the hawk off the high wall.' The collected / Bounty she dispenses: kind particulars . . . / 'Everything serves to further.' Deliverance. The moon / There, then there, then there, now here: its white light spread / Over a Gotham winterscape—the while the new song / Gets itself composed for life: another wayfarer . . .

"Collected together, enlightened, let's from hence

spread / Particulars of this news—publish this song: / Moon, addressed as woman, still directs each way- farer . . ."

"Bravo!" cried Boadicea Tillinghast, voicing the general consensus.

"It's TIME we called for our taxi," Mawrdew Czgowchwz whispered to Kaye Wayfaring.

Mawrdew Czgowchwz shuttered the windows and drew the drapes against the winter nightscape of Gramercy Park, then turned back to her guest.

"I sat riveted, reading Jameson's account of your precip- itous Clayton journey, then barreled along uptown with- out fastening and curtaining like a proper Irishwoman is directed to do. '*Privvicy* from the inside out, and *privvicy* from the outside in!' "

"The way they did in Clayton. Up at the Dakota, before the show, I read your letter again—with the drapes open, so that I could see the Park, and remember."

"I sat where you're sitting now, writing it, driven to inaugurate something—whatever."

"I'm afraid I have an embarrassing question to put to you."

"Sought-after guests, especially on first visits, are enti- tled to embarrassing questions."

"Where is it kept?"

"Where is it— Oh, the Academy Award. It's right there. And I can assure you, in spite of what you may have heard, it did not come sailing in the window."

The diva pointed across the room to a rounded corner niche (atop a junction of deep shelves containing numbers of vocal scores) in which in demi-shadow stood the slender gold statue.

I must not go up to it, Kaye Wayfaring told herself. What must I do? I must call the curse by name. I must talk about the feeling, say something presentable.

"I keep asking myself how important can it be, after all?"

"After all, almost certainly not at all, but we are so queerly constituted: I seem to remember there was a time I thought 'I could kill someone for it.'"

"I used to dream I had committed murder."

"And won a prize?"

"They gave me the Academy Award and the gas chamber. I could not convince that jury that I'd only been acting."

"Shall I do tea? The boarder will take some when he traipses in. Make yourself comfortable. Throw another log on the fire."

ALONE again, Kaye Wayfaring rehearsed her situation. How had everything happened? She put another log on the fire and sat back to reverie.

Let's see: He fell off the horse. . . . He came around again the next day. . . . I made a point of not teasing him. . . . He started making sketches the way Jameson does. . . . He and Jameson seemed so close; I asked him about it by way of getting acquainted. . . . "Jameson says it started when we were young. He says he said to Mother, 'You've got two and I've got none, so I'll take one.'" . . . I told him I remembered them both from *Macbeth*, prompted by the letter. . . . We resumed playing pinochle. . . . It came out he was playing hookey the whole time, although he insisted I couldn't call it hookey: it was a leave. . . . I said, "Don't try to snow me, Mister, you're A.W.O.L." . . . And he answered, "Fujigmo." . . . " 'Fujigmo?' Where did you learn 'Fujigmo'? My brother always said 'Fujigmo'!" I continued asking the questions like that and he continued answering the questions. . . . He answered every question. . . . We finished at the Central Park location. . . . He and his brother went away together to some undisclosed location: which they declare is a thing they plan to do from time to time for the rest of their lives.

He came to *Twelfth Night* second night, third night, closing night. . . . We walked along the beach all night and watched the sun come up over Georgica Pond. . . . Everything I said to him he seemed to understand, which I told him I considered impossible. . . . He said nothing, and kept drawing stars with seven points in the sand with a stick.

I had always known that men were crudely explicit, only this one wasn't. . . . Of course he wasn't a man, was he, he was a boy, wasn't he, I reasoned. . . . That's what I said, I reasoned. I thought I could reason. . . . Meanwhile, he was a twin and his twin was my dearest chum's lover. . . . "I never have," he told me. . . . "Why tell me that?" I asked him. . . . "I don't know: to let you off the hook, I guess, if you feel hooked. It seems I do."

We went swimming, then ducked into the summerhouse and sat shivering without a stitch on. . . . "I don't do this kind of thing," I said to him. . . . "I never have, I told you, but it doesn't appear to me I can stop now. You can, though." . . . So I took him up on it, and here I am.

The host re-entered, carrying a tea tray.

"Let me help," said Kaye, sitting halfway up in the chair.

"No, stay there; I'll be mother."

"That's pretty funny, really."

"The boys think I'm a riot, and aren't given to cloaking that opinion."

"I've never heard—"

"No, he wouldn't. He's timid about disclosing much of the intelligence he's arrived at prompted by the troublesome one, the private investigator."

"I was just sitting here thinking about how what's happened happened."

"Any luck? Milk, no sugar, isn't it?"

"No—yes, that's right."

"Well, sleep on it, and we'll talk it over tomorrow, if you like, on the ride up to Manitoy."

"Tomorrow—another day."

"And there's no getting away from it when you're Irish."

"You are funny—and you make the best tea. You can be my mother any time."

"Agreeing to pay the withholding tax due to metaphor, I'll take the job."

"I decided I couldn't possibly make a picture based on my mother's diary."

"I can't be sorry for that."

"There's a picture there all right, but not for me."

"Not every possible picture should be made."

"Not every possible face should be shown to the world?"

"Not, at any rate, to the world assembled."

"Well, then, what about the one where I play you, pregnant, singing *La Fanciulla del West* at Covent Garden and making the picture in Ireland about *your* mother?"

"That came up earlier," Mawrdew Czgowchwz allowed. "Madge is vehement against."

"She doesn't think I have the wherewithal to play you, and she's right."

"On this score, she doesn't think, she feels—hordes galloping over her grave to buy tickets to a spectacle she couldn't attend."

"Not every possible spectacle should be produced?"

"I, of course, couldn't like anything more. Look at you! You're ravishingly beautiful, in your prime, a great, billowing vessel of womanhood. They'd use all the old tapes, laundered, technologically state-of-the-arted. . . . Looking like you and sounding like that, I'd go out and drop dead on the sidewalk, beatified—*sanctified!*"

"Well, that's that," Kaye Wayfaring said. "Let's talk about heredity."

"Shall I commence telling you some of the things that happened back then?"

"I sometimes think that's one of the reasons I let all this happen—just to hear."

"It's some saga, all right, but then whose isn't, all told, after all?"

"I'll settle for yours. I've been hanging around forever waiting to hear it."

Mawrdew Czgowchwz started telling Kaye Wayfaring everything that had gone on. . . .

THE SPARROWS' morning noises on the dayward side of the drawn drapes and bolted shutters were suddenly counterpointed by the sound of two identical voices in the outer hall, and, as Mawrdew Czgowchwz rose to pull the drape cord and undo the latches, her twin sons entered the room.

"He was stuck on a bridge in Connecticut," Tristan Beltane said.

"And this part you won't believe," said Jacob. "We were stuck on the bridge at Cos Cob, and in the bridge house the bridgeman was looking at television, so that through the window of the train, for almost two hours, I watched *We Are Born, We Live, We Die.*"

All in one day. No. I must stop thinking that.

"From Atlanta. I saw it listed in the *Times,*" said Mawrdew Czgowchwz, admitting the morning sun. "Well, you got here. Say hello."

"Hello," Jacob said to Kaye, sitting down at her feet.

"Hello. This is a surprise."

"I couldn't stay up there another night looking at that lighthouse."

"And I can't stay awake another minute."

SHE LAY in bed alone, remembering everything.

It would make some picture, though. Absolutely.

I must try to get some sleep. Those two whispering away next door: it's as if they were spelling one another's cues.

What a story: everything: the bloodhounds, the police, the warlock . . . the Irish called him that: a misnomer. All hers: then them in there, one of whom is now mine to call. I won't: I'll leave him talking with his brother.

Twins are terribly sexy. . . . I can't think about that. If I think about that, I'll go nuts for sure. I can't think: I must just sleep. . . . Later today we'll leave for Manitoy, and up there I'll sleep into tomorrow, and whatever, whatever there is to think about, I'll think about it tomorrow. After all, tomorrow is another day.

A NOTE ON THE TYPE

This book was set in a digitized version of Janson, a typeface recut for
Linotype direct from type cast from matrices long thought to have
been made by the Dutchman Anton Janson, who was a practicing type
founder in Leipzig during the years 1668–1687. However, it has been
conclusively demonstrated that these types are actually the work of
Nicholas Kis (1650–1702), a Hungarian, who most probably learned his
trade from the master Dutch type founder Dirk Voskens. The type
is an excellent example of the influential and sturdy Dutch types that
prevailed in England up to the time William Caslon (1692–1766) devel-
oped his own incomparable designs from them.

Composed, printed and bound by
The Haddon Craftsmen, Inc.,
Scranton, Pennsylvania.

Designed by Virginia Tan.